To ordinary, everyday reality. You were always there when I needed you.

Moody Gets the Blues

Moody Gets the Blues

By
Steve Oliver

OffByOne Press

ISBN 0-9644138-7-6
Library of Congress Catalog Card Number: 96-092218
FIRST PRINTING

All of the events and characters
depicted in this book are fictional.

Illustrations by the author.

April, 1978

CHAPTER ONE

The cab barreled down Division Street. My passenger, a drunken Unitarian, slumped in the back seat. An April rain streaked the windows and blackened the street. It was two a.m. and I was just beginning to wake up.

It had been a slow night so far, but business was improving as the bars let out and I ushered the usual drunks to their sleazy dumps or South Hill mansions. Their destinations were usually predicted by the quality of bar they oozed out of. This one had come from a singles party over in Browne's Addition before he landed in Ode's Bar and Grill with a bag on. At least that's what he had mumbled in the first few minutes he was in the cab before lapsing into narcolepsy. I believed him. You find that people in cabs usually tell the truth; it's just that you'd rather not hear it.

1

Even if I had normally cared about my passengers, I wouldn't have on this occasion. I was preoccupied because the city had issued me my private investigator's license earlier in the day. I had applied months earlier and then forgotten about the license until they called and told me it had been approved.

I plucked the license out of my pocket and looked at it again. It was just fine except for the picture.

The stamp-sized photo had been taken shortly after I got out of the mental hospital. In the photo I still looked a little bewildered, as though someone had just asked me for my 1976 tax returns. My hair had not been washed that day and hung down in long strings. Then there was my face—wide-set gray eyes, a square jaw, a nose that looked like it had been broken a dozen times. It was a rough—some said good-looking—face topped by black hair and distinguished by a mustache showing a few gray hairs. Other people seemed to like it, but I couldn't stand it, and I seldom used a mirror even to shave.

The document itself was perfect—the official signatures, the thumbprint, were just the way I wanted them. I smiled with satisfaction, but not for long because ahead of me a truck was backing onto the street. I could have stopped in time, but instead I jumped lanes, much to the surprise of the driver of a decaying Volkswagen with one headlight that was already occupying the lane. He honked his horn, a pointless lament, before he ducked into oncoming traffic, then fell in behind me. My Unitarian dropped from sight in the back as I cleared the truck by a full inch and pulled into the right lane. I follow the customs of the road, so I shook my fist at the truck driver and blew a kiss to the Volkswagen as it passed, engine screaming. The driver stuck his hand out the window in a one-finger salute. I turned right onto Mission, the wide, tree-lined boulevard that bisects Spokane's near north side.

I woke my fare at his house and he dragged himself off the floor of the car muttering something about cab drivers and single women. I didn't get the connection and I didn't care.

I took his five-dollar bill and watched as he stumbled up the steps to the walkway to his door. He drifted over the edge of his lawn, landing on a shrub. If I had been a gardener it would have bothered me.

On the way downtown I called in and the dispatcher directed me to the Galley, a north-side seafood house.

It was closed, of course, and I found all the doors locked. I wouldn't wait long for this one, but hung around a bit to see if a fare would materialize. After a few minutes a very pretty blond about twenty-five years old walked out. She would have been under contract to Paramount if they did that sort of thing anymore. She had the symmetrical features they looked for—blue eyes, polite nose, full lips. Her golden hair was perfectly styled, the end of the hairdo bouncing just an inch or so above the collar of her tan trench coat. I couldn't tell that much about her body under the coat, but the look of her legs as she got into my cab gave me something to think about.

"Hi," she said as she closed the cab door. It was the "hi" of a sweet kid from the suburbs—of someone whose family ate together in the dining room amid pleasant conversation. The orthodontically corrected teeth glowed bright white in the mercury-lamp light of the parking lot. She was the first sober customer I'd had in hours. I nodded my reply.

"Take me to 1524 West Alameda," she said, and I pulled out of the parking lot. That would put me on the South Hill, away from the bars and most of the fares, but that was okay for a while.

"So, how do you like the Galley?" I asked, just passing time as we pulled onto the street.

"So-so," she replied, "I work there."

"Oh."

"It's okay. I like working with people." She was looking at me now, studying me, I guess. It's a funny thing about a lot of women—the moment they find out you don't give a shit you suddenly become interesting. "We're in the same business," she continued, "dealing with people, I mean."

"Most of my fares aren't people."

"Well, thanks," she said, and laughed.

"I didn't mean you, of course."

"Can I ask you something personal?" A coy intimacy entered her voice.

"Sure."

"Did you break your nose or something?"

"That happened when I was about twelve," I told her. "I guess I thought I was tough because I picked a fight with a guy named Buell. I mean, a guy with a name like Buell shouldn't be able to fight, should he? Anyway, he kicked hell out of me. My parents didn't realize it was broken, I guess, because it healed this way." Geez, what a story—Buell yet. I wondered if she'd buy it.

In fact, she laughed. "Well, it's all right. It makes you attractive in a rough sort of way."

We were passing downtown. The cab swung right at Second Street, heading west to the arterial that climbed the South Hill. As I pulled up to her apartment building she was writing something on a small card. She handed it to me with her fare. Her name, Rhonda, and a phone number were written on the card.

"Call me sometime," she said.

"What for?"

"Just call me sometime." She got out of the cab. "Good night."

After I was back on the street I looked at the card for a moment. I reached into the pocket of my denim shirt and pulled out the other four cards I had been given during the past week. Mary, Susan, Audrey, Kim, and now Rhonda. What was the world coming to when you couldn't just quietly be a scummy cab driver without being bothered by a bunch of women? You'd have to be nice to them, and buy them things, and then sooner or later they would expect you to sleep with them. I certainly wasn't looking forward to that. I gathered the cards and threw them out the window. It was a nice neighborhood. Maybe some nice guy would find the cards and give them a call.

I punched the play button on the cassette recorder that would come in handy for my PI cases, and the soft strains of Beethoven's Fifth filled the cab. I waited patiently for the music to switch to the bouncy rock of ELO's "Roll Over Beethoven," and I jumped all over the cab on the way back to the stand.

It was after eight in the morning when I got off work with a fairly good night's take, at least for cabbing in Spokane. It's a nice little city, but it's not exactly a world-class financial hub. To those of us who grew up here it's a friendly, unpretentious little town. It has to be unpretentious because nobody knows it exists. It's an inland city at the center of a vast area that used to be pretty uninhabited, and is now sparsely populated. The area is called the Inland Empire, and I guess that Spokane is its hub. It's an area where Indians roamed freely for a long time, even after the railroad came through and began to spoil things for them. The town is bigger now, but it still has that straightforward frontier town feel. It's a much better place to live than New York or Los Angeles—hell-holes full of snobs, shady characters, filth, and hostility, where a cynic like me would get lost in the crowd. Here, I'm unique.

Normally after a twelve-hour shift I would have gone immediately to bed, but this time I planned to phone the lawyer as soon as I got back to my apartment. I call it my apartment for the benefit of polite society that might not understand living in a seventy-five dollar dump, especially if you don't mind it all that much. The place is located in a light industrial area of Spokane to the east of Division Street where all the dislocated old people, blacks, and cabbies reside. Those buildings that still house people rather than cars, lumber, or machinery parts are mostly eighty-year-old brick affairs that were converted to indoor plumbing sometime during the 1930s. My apartment is one of a row of apartments in a single-story building with some commercial concerns—worries might better describe them—still hanging on. There's an occult book store just down from me, and my place had been an incense shop back when that sort of thing was novel and "underground." Now it's a three-room horror repainted bright yellow, with a flowered linoleum floor that is turning to dust. But it's mine alone, and after the hospital that's something I need. I especially like the skylights, which had probably been industrial chimneys at one time. I also like the views—there are two—one of the beer trucks going by in the morning, and the other, in the rear, of a pile of discarded tire carcasses from the Ace Rubber Company.

The pile of tires is kind of comforting. My life is like one of those tires. I threw it on the trash heap in the same way. It's 1978, after all, and things are strange for everyone. The Vietnam war is over. There's no longer a division between hippies and straight people since everyone is wearing bizarre clothes—leisure suits, bell-bottom pants, paisley shirts, platform shoes. A peanut farmer is president and he has a brother, Billy Carter, selling Billy Beer. By 1978 I am no longer a hippie, but I haven't gone entirely straight either. I joined another club. I'm a cab driver—which in Spokane in 1978 means I'm basically scum. I've thrown my life on the trash heap, like it was one of those bald tires with threads showing through. And it's comforting to be so far down that failure is no longer an issue. I'm kind of enjoying it.

As I entered my apartment I almost knocked over Irving. He's a philodendron who resides on the table by the front window. He passed away two months ago when I was first out of the hospital and not doing too well at taking care of other living things. He's now mummified by the dry air of the living room which is superheated by the oil stove. I keep him mostly for sentimental reasons, feeling a certain guilt over his death. I carefully brushed him off and pushed him toward the center of the table. Then I picked up the phone and dialed the number.

It was after nine a.m. and the lawyer should have arrived within the past few minutes. *What a weird time to be getting to work*, I thought.

"Brownwell, Casdorff, and Goodie," the secretary chirped. "May I help you?"

"Is Nat Goodie in?"

"Who is calling, please?"

"Scott Moody."

"I'll connect you."

"Moody," said Nat when he came on the line. "What's happenin', man?" Nat talked like this because it's 1978 and we are all watching too much *Starsky and Hutch*. Everyone thinks being a streetwise black is probably the coolest thing there is—even a lawyer with horn-rimmed glasses. I had met Nat one night when I picked him up at a whorehouse on Spokane's east side. Though he was from another social class, he was pretty convivial, partly because he had been drinking. He was about five-nine, but otherwise a big man—filling out his wool three-piece suit. He told me he was a lawyer from New York and had been in Spokane ten years. I told him I was interested in the law because I wanted to be a PI. The topic came up again because after that I kept running into him, often at the same east-side address. After a while, perhaps under the influence of liquor, he relented and agreed to let me have a shot at some work if I got my license.

"I'm looking for a case," I told him. "I got my PI license yesterday. I have my business license."

"Well, congratulations. You know, being a PI in Spokane isn't all that exciting. You ain't gonna be no Shaft."

"I don't wanta be no Shaft. I just want a little case to get me started."

"I've got some subpoenas to serve, an eviction or

8

two."

"Just what I wanted."

"I'll try to find you something better, but we've already got a firm that handles our investigations. Drop by in the afternoon. I'll give you some papers to serve."

I hung up the phone and walked to the kitchen. To do that I had to go through my bedroom, which was the middle room of the apartment. It was a small room that had no doors. I looked at the bed, a disheveled mess of blankets on a mattress I had thrown in the corner. Some day I'll wash the sheets, make the bed, then I'll take pictures.

I fixed myself a strong cup of coffee, turned on the TV, and went to bed. I have to have coffee to sleep. The game show I watched was less essential, though I do need to listen to something as I go to sleep—radio or TV, I don't care. Bad as TV can be, it's better than letting down my guard and ending up listening to the voices in my head.

I woke at about four, right in the middle of a TV western. I propped myself up in bed and smoked a cigarette. I tried to figure out what the hell movie this was.

Dan Blocker was in it, dressed up to look like a hayseed. He used to play "Hoss" on *Bonanza*. He's dead now—heart attack. Wally Cox was playing the local businessman. I'm not sure, but I think he had a heart attack too. It's so depressing watching dead people walk around talking and having a good time like they were doing something besides remaining very still and holding their breath. I switched it off and turned on the radio.

At a little after five that afternoon I dropped by Nat's office to pick up the papers—two of them—from his secretary. She handed them to me and at the same time pushed a button on the intercom. "Mr. Moody is here," she said. A moment later Nat came out of his office. As usual he was in a three-piece suit that had been let out to accommodate his spreading waistline and he was holding an unlit cigar.

"Hey, Moody, just one thing—no hassles. Just serve the papers and get out of there. These people aren't pussycats."

I reported to the garage at six and signed out forty-one, my favorite car. I liked it because the door handles worked.

That evening, a Friday, was busier than my previous shift. One of my first customers was Poet Bob. Poet Bob was sixtyish and had a gray beard, little beady bloodshot eyes, a red nose and a flaccid little potbelly under a dirty plaid work shirt. He was wearing his usual trench coat that looked like it had been run over by a herd of cattle, and a cap, the kind they wore during the Depression—which had lasted a little longer for Poet Bob than for everyone else.

He carried a soiled duffel bag and was heading for Hillyard, a run-down area of town that was the butt of a lot of Polish-type jokes. He always claimed to be planning to catch a boxcar for Montana. I had been taking him to Hillyard for this purpose for a couple of months now, but he never managed to get out of town. Every few days I would pick him up at Andy's or the Purple Onion or some other wino dive and he would head for Hillyard. I couldn't help wondering how he ever got back downtown.

As Bob got out of the car and paid the fare, he

told me, "You're a prince of a lad, really you are. You've a good sense of driving, even *this* car. Stay the course, don't be a clown, save up your money, then get the hell out of town."

Poet Bob gave good advice.

I headed south and picked up a guy at a bowling alley who wanted to find a hooker. When they were both in the car—the bald guy whose wife thought he was in a league, and the black prostitute with a fur coat and wig—they began discussing places to go and "do it." She didn't want to go to his brother's apartment and he didn't want to go to her place. He didn't want to spend his money on a rented room. Finally, as we drove around town, they started to do it in the back of the cab.

"Hey, you two," I told them, "I don't care what you do back there, but there's a five dollar entertainment fee and you have to be neat."

So we drove around on the back streets with them ruining the shocks. At one point during the proceedings I felt the prostitute's hand caressing the back of my head and I had to lean forward to drive. As the hooker got out of the car on Main Street, she leaned over to my ear and said, "Baby, why don't you give me a call sometime when we're both off duty?" and she gave me her phone number. Later I would post it on the bulletin board at the cab lot.

At about six a.m. I called the dispatcher and told him I had some errands to run before I turned in the car, so he signed me off the air and I headed for my first delivery for Nat.

The address on the eviction Nat had given me was an apartment house on Third Avenue, a rundown racially mixed area not far from my place. I pulled up in front at about six-fifteen and left the car running. I was going about this according to the advice of a PI acquaintance of a few years earlier. He said if you serve subpoenas and eviction notices early in the morning when people still aren't functioning, they aren't as likely to give you a bloody nose.

The building was a brick one with a wooden porch that squeaked as I crossed it to the door, which, naturally, was wide open—no security buildings in slums. I walked down the hall, taking in the dim lighting and musty smells. There were still some places I would not have called home.

I stopped at 107. I paused a moment, then knocked on the door—loud. I heard some thumping around inside, then the door opened and there was a black guy about ten feet tall standing in the opening. He had a gun in his hand.

"What can I do for you?" I asked.

"You can get the hell out of this building."

"I must have the wrong apartment. I thought a friend of mine lived here—James Leach."

"You ain't no friend of mine."

I dropped the eviction notice and ran like hell for the front door. He yelled at me, but I figured certain rules of etiquette could be suspended in the presence of a gun and I did not answer. I bolted through the doorway, jumped into the cab, and removed several teeth from its gears getting away from there.

I drove north for my second call. This time it was a small ranch-style house near the Spokane River and I felt a little better about it. This was a subpoena, not an eviction, and in a nice neighborhood so it might be okay. The sun was coming up and there was a nice smell in the air. A man in his late thirties came to the door after I rang the bell for a few minutes.

He was about my height, six feet, with dark, wildly tousled hair, a pencil mustache, and a face showing signs of water retention. He was wearing a velour robe and smoking a cigarette. He seemed dazed and confused. It looked like my plan was working this time.

"Are you Mr. Ralph Schumsky?"

"Uh, wait, yes, that's right."

I handed him the subpoena. "Here you go," I said. He looked at the document, then let it drop to the ground.

That's when he punched me. Right in the nose. Jesus, not the nose again. I reeled backward, and staggered off the lawn to the cab. I'd had enough of these easy cases. I wanted something tough.

"How you doin', Moody?" the voice over the phone asked.

"Dot doo bad," I answered, holding the cold compress to my nose. "Gedding lods of resd."

"I hear you had a little trouble serving the papers."

"The usual. Bud the guy god my noze."

"So I heard. What ever happened to that nose anyway? It's obvious you aren't a boxer."

"Doh. Car wreg. Hid the sdeering wheel."

"Oh. Say, the reason I called is, I've got some work for you. When you're feeling okay."

"Wad me to drop by?"

"Anytime this week. No rush. Interesting case—a missing person. I thought you might be good because you see a lot of the town. You just might pick him up off the street."

"Yeah, cud habben."

"Aren't you going to ask me about money?"

"I'b a cab driver, rebeber. I'b a philanthrobist." I hung up the phone.

A missing person. That was a little more like it. I sat at the table. I took the only writing instrument in the house, a vermilion crayon I had found beneath the stove, and began to design a business card with the name of my new firm: Moody Investigations.

It was Wednesday night before I felt well enough to go back to work and Thursday morning when I dropped in on Nat. As usual, he was with a client, so I sat in the waiting room alternating between sleep and consciousness. It's difficult to stay awake on 600 milligrams of Thorazine unless you have a really good reason. They had given me the prescription for Thorazine when I left the hospital—insisted upon it in fact. I didn't object. I wanted the Thorazine. Thorazine was my security. Thorazine was my life. It wasn't so much that Thorazine made me sane or even prevented the pain that had been attendant to choosing sanity. It just dulled me out so I really wasn't bothered by much of anything.

When I was awake I was thinking about Nat. I wondered what his full first name was. Natalusious? Natatorious? Natwood? That was a possibility. Natwick? Maybe. Nathaniel? Nathaniel. That was probably it. How boring. That was the way my mind worked anymore—I'd had a lot of memory burned out. It would come up with the wildest speculation and I would have to keep calculating to get closer to normal brain functioning. When I finally tracked my way through the maze to the center, the more likely answer usually turned out to be something really boring, like Nathaniel.

I was nodding off for the third time, dreaming about Nathaniel Hawthorne, when the receptionist shook me, then pulled her hand back as though she had just touched a slug.

"Mr. Goodie can see you now," she said. *Though I don't know why,* she might have added. She was a middle-fifties matron who stared at me out of thick glasses to see if I was going to come out of my trance. I focused on her graying bouffant hairdo.

"Thanks, sister." I rose and walked into Nat's office.

It was a nice office—lots of hardwood paneling and expensive art and furniture that gave the impression he was doing well and you ought to check your fly. I took a seat in the leather chair he motioned me to. Nat was wearing a three-piece pinstripe and he was smoking a cigar that cost more than my car. The entire tableau reminded me that I needed to think about what kind of fee I was going to charge.

"You don't look as bad as I expected," said Nat, tapping ash from his cigar and exposing a fine gold watch on his wrist. "Your nose doesn't look much worse for the wear."

"I'm okay."

"I told you when we met that being a PI wouldn't be a picnic."

"I hate picnics."

Nat chuckled, grinned the big grin. "Man, you got a reply for everything." He put his cigar in the ashtray and moved some documents nearer to indicate he was ready to get down to business.

"Well, we'll have some more papers for you to

serve, but right now I've got an ongoing case you can work on. Part of the reason I'm giving you the case is because you're the only one I know who'll work this cheap. But if you can find the guy, you get a bonus."

"What's the rate?" I picked up the crystal figurine from the desk and studied it as though I was interested.

"Keep track of your hours. We'll give you twenty an hour plus reasonable expenses. There's limited travel, but very limited. If you want to go somewhere to check out a lead you'd better have a good reason for it. This is a nice lady you're working for and I want to treat her right."

I nodded.

"Her name is Deirdre Mercer. Her husband disappeared three months ago. The police have worked on it, but I suspect not as hard as they could. You might check with them and see what they've found out. We had a detective look for him, but he did the conventional things—which I don't think will work in this case. Talk to that guy to make sure you don't repeat the effort." Goodie handed me a business card. "The rest of the information you can get from the guy's wife and his friends. You know the rules, now you'll have to learn the ropes. Don't embarrass me, okay?"

"I think I can handle it," I said, wondering where the hell I would look for someone who was missing.

"I hope so. I'm giving you a break. Don't screw it up. The paperwork's in here," he said, indicating a pile of documents in a manila file folder. "Take care of it with Marge before you leave. She'll have you sign an agreement specifying the terms of your employment."

"Okay."

"You're bonded, aren't you?"

"As of yesterday," I lied.

"Do you have an accountant?"

"No."

"I'll give you a name," he said, scribbling it on the manila folder. "You'll need one if you last."

"Thanks, Nat," I said, taking the folder.

"Anytime, Moody."

I started toward Marge's desk.

"By the way."

"Yeah."

"Get some clothes, okay?"

I looked at my jeans and work shirt. "What for?"

Nat gave me a pained look. "This is a classy lady. I don't want her to think I'm sending her a cab driver."

I decided to start work that day, so when I got home I called my client and made an appointment to see her that afternoon. I used my business voice and business name. Then, after I had slept a few hours, I shaved, took a shower, and changed into my best clothes—a corduroy sports jacket I had picked up at a thrift shop and a pair of polyester slacks left over from a former life. Then I put on my blue and white sneakers.

I hoped she wouldn't notice.

I drove up the South Hill in my Pinto to the address Nat had given me. As usual when I was in my Pinto, I kept my eye on the rearview mirror. You never know when some bike is going to crash into you and set you on fire. It was a crummy little car but I was very proud of it. A local finance company had actually agreed to give me credit so I could buy it, and I was so happy about being trusted that I didn't mind paying Las Vegas interest.

The neighborhood my client lived in had been built during the 1920s and 1930s by local doctors and dentists who used lots of oak and walnut and beams you could crack your wrecking ball on. The number I stopped at was a three-story Tudor with leaded-glass windows. It had been nicely cared for. A Mercedes and a Cadillac were parked on the stone driveway. On second thought I decided to park down the street so I wouldn't be associated with my car. Pintos are more suited to roller derby matches than the South Hill.

I rang the doorbell and shifted my weight from one foot to the other for a couple of years waiting for someone to answer. I held the sheaf of papers under my arm and had my recorder slung over my right shoulder. Oddly, I felt like having a cigarette. I normally never smoke unless I'm going to bed or getting up.

The door, a big solid-oak affair with a knocker, finally swung open. And there she stood. The name on the driver's license may have been Deirdre Mercer, but she was Deirdre O'Connell to me.

CHAPTER TWO

She was quite a different Deirdre than I remembered. Older, naturally. Blonder now, and upswept in the elegant style of ladies in the ads in *The New Yorker*. The eyes were still brown, though, and she was still slim. Her breasts, as best I could discern them through the blue-gray turtleneck, had filled out. A single gold chain hung around her neck and she had gold studs in her earlobes. Expensive wool slacks draped loosely over her hips. She was dressed the way I imagined well-off housewives dressed when they walked their poodles. With all her good looks and cute buck teeth, there was something hard about her, as there had been when we dated—ebony beneath the velvet. She could be fun one moment, then, when the subject was money or religion, turn stony if I said something irreverent. But, even in those moments, she was sexy. She exuded sex. W*hat's she up to now?*, I wondered. Was she Nat's playmate? Probably not. He had the money, but he had a curious propensity for whore-houses.

Thinking of her, and of those times, I began to get dizzy and felt a rush of emotion—fear, sorrow, nostalgia, panic, passed through my body. Partly this was due to the Thorazine which caused low blood pressure. When I was driving cab I had to be careful whenever I was required to get out of the car. Each time I would have to lean on the taxi's door for a moment while I blacked out as my blood pressure adjusted to standing up. Just now, in her doorway, I thought I might quietly faint.

She was looking at me questioningly, and I thought she recognized me, but then I saw the look was more general, meaning, *What the hell are you doing on my doorstep, and would you hurry the hell up?*

"Yes?" she asked finally.

"Mrs. Mercer?"

"That's right."

"I'm the investigator. I called earlier."

"Oh, yes. Won't you come in? Sorry about the mess," she said as she ushered me into an immaculate living room. The nearest thing to a mess was a half-finished drink next to an open decanter.

The place looked like one of the fancy show-rooms at upper-class furniture stores—the kind that wouldn't let me in the door unless I had a hand-truck. There were white rugs and glass coffee tables and cute little stainless steel lamps standing around. She offered me a place on a huge sofa facing a fireplace that could have housed four Santas. Paintings on the wall fairly beamed ostentation. Deirdre O'Connell was a long way from that college sophomore I had known fifteen years ago.

"Would you like a drink?" she asked as she walked toward the decanter of whiskey. She wanted to continue drinking, but drinking without offering would be impolite.

"Sure."

"Scotch all right?"

"Fine."

She got a glass from the bar at the other side of the room and poured half a glass, neat.

When she was seated, way down the couch at the other end, I pointed to the recorder. "Do you mind if I turn this on while we talk? I'd like to have a record."

"That's all right," she said, slurring her words. She lifted her drink to her lips and drank like it was going to save her life. I could see now why she didn't recognize me—she was very drunk. I had seen a lot of people like this when I was selling— people who could drink and drink and drink, and if you didn't know them you wouldn't immediately know that they were out of touch with their surroundings. I didn't want her to recognize me. I didn't want to discuss what I had become, so it was all right with me.

I punched the button on my recorder, ran through a little preamble, then placed the recorder between us. "I understand your husband has been missing for the past three months," I said, "and you want me to try to find him."

"He's been gone nearly four. Yes, I want someone to find him. The police have done little enough. And that *damned* detective." She lit a cigarette with the big lighter on the coffee table. Her hands were exquisite. No baby fat these days.

"Tell me about the circumstances of Mr. Mercer's

disappearance."

"There weren't any. One day he left to go to work and he never came home. He didn't go to work either, as far as I know. No one at the office saw him. Later, they did find his car a few blocks away—the Mercedes."

"Where did he work?" I still felt like having a cigarette, but I never carry them and I didn't want to ask for one of hers. She smoked Salems.

"We own a real estate office downtown. Actually we own several, but that's the main one, Mercer Manor, Inc." She was not smiling about her good fortune. The beautiful face was pouting. She reached for the decanter on the table again and refilled her glass. In the old days she would have passed out after drinking one bottle of beer.

"Can you give me a couple of contacts at work—people I can talk to about his disappearance?"

"Yes." She gave me the names and I jotted them down.

"There was nothing unusual before his disappearance then? No change in mood, no indication he might be in some kind of trouble?"

She lit another cigarette. She had two of them going now, one in her hand and the other in the big glass ashtray. Soon, I was sure, she would light a third and a fourth and I would be forced to smoke Salems just because of their increasing availability.

"He seemed a bit distant," she said. "But it's been that way for a long time." The smoke drifted out of her beautiful nose and mouth. It rose and I found myself distracted by it; I watched as it lifted toward the high white ceiling among the wooden beams. It joined a cirrus cloud of cigarette smoke floating above us. "There is one thing I wanted to tell you though," she said.

"Oh, what was that?"

"I think Wendell is still around. I don't think he's been kidnapped or hurt or anything."

"Why not?"

"Because the house was broken into last week and a couple of his favorite things are missing."

What could that be, I wondered, *his favorite money clip? his rubber ducky?*

"Nothing else?"

"No. And the house wasn't actually broken into. Someone had a key."

"So you think that it was Wendell—that he's hiding out here in town?"

"I'm sure of it. It would be just like him to do that." There was a bitter edge to her voice that was new to me. She had hurt and been hurt a lot. It was strange, but it was the first time during the interview I actually felt attracted to her.

"What was missing?" I was looking at her eyes. For some perverse reason I was trying to get her to recognize me, to acknowledge me.

"Five of his books and a camera. Also an electric razor."

Five books? This guy was as exciting as Jimmy Carter. "How did you happen to notice?"

She put out both of her current cigarettes and lit a new one. This time she was looking at me and I thought I saw a flicker of recognition. "I just noticed is all. I check that sort of thing."

I wouldn't have wanted her for a boss at inventory time. The sound of that last statement was a little off key, but I let it pass. "Why books?"

"Why not books?" She curled her legs beneath her on the couch and settled back. "He collected books." She looked down into her drink, contemplating something. "It's odd, though."

"What's odd?"

"The books he took. I wouldn't have thought they were his type."

"What were they?"

"Children's books, with lots of illustrations—by Wyeth, I think, and someone else. They were nice, but he was into more literary fare."

Big deal. With a lead like that I could find my way to the front door. I decided there was little more to do here, and the distance between me and Deirdre was greater than the fifteen years that had passed. She wouldn't have given me a tumble if I'd been with Barnum and Bailey.

"Do you have a picture or two I could take? Something recent."

"I was planning on giving you baby pictures," she said acidly. "Of course I have pictures. Just a minute, I'll get them." She rose and drifted out of the room. I suddenly felt like an encyclopedia salesman on a cold call. I got up and wandered behind the couch and loitered there trying to get my slacks to cover my sneakers.

She returned with the photographs. One of them had been badly mauled. She did not like being crossed and Wendell had crossed her. The mauled photo was of Deirdre and Wendell on some happier occasion. They were standing, arms around one another, a drink in hand, a swimming pool in the background, and they were smiling at the photographer. The time of day was twilight. Wendell had the moronic, disingenuous smile I would expect of a realtor. He had thick brown hair that covered his ears, and long sideburns. He also had a mustache.

I wondered if maybe I ought to shave mine off. In 1978 it seemed like every idiot had a mustache.

I looked back at the picture, studying Mercer's

face. It was almost perfectly square and he wore a set of heavy glasses that magnified his eyes a little. Deirdre must have married him for love, because it wasn't for looks. And not for his body either—he was a little pudgy around his white belt and maroon pants.

The second photo was a black and white, just an eight-by-ten headshot, probably for business purposes. Were those small dart holes in the picture or was that my imagination? Well, no matter.

"These will be fine," I said. "Can you tell me what he was wearing when you last saw him?"

"Yes, if you think he hasn't changed clothes in the past three months." She was standing beside me now, behind the couch, her newly poured drink in hand, and she was leaning toward the door.

"Yeah. Well, I don't suppose it's too important." I remembered my tape recorder and punched the stop button, picked it up off the couch, and started for the door. She drifted behind me.

"One more thing," I said as I neared the doorway. "Why do you want your husband back? It sounds like an odd question, but I'd like to know."

"Why do you think? He's my husband. He belongs here."

"You're not worried about him though." I leaned against the doorknob waiting for her answer.

"Not really. I was until last week, but not now. I don't know why he left and I'm not sure I want to know. I just want him back."

"Any legal reasons?"

"Well, he has left things a little ambiguous, if that's what you mean. Some things were in his name only."

"I see." I opened the door and started out. "I'll call you," I said, "if anything turns up."

"I'll be holding my breath until I hear from you."

"Yeah." I walked out and the big door thudded behind me. What fun. So much for any romantic notions I had harbored during the intervening years. I had evidently remembered her a lot better than she had remembered me. Between the booze, the years, and the nose, she didn't know who the hell I was. Whatever the reason, I was glad that she didn't seem to know me. I wanted an anonymous client, not a former girlfriend who would notice the kind of scum I had turned out to be. Maybe I could find her husband without having to see her again.

I walked down to the Pinto, got in, and promptly fell asleep behind the wheel. I woke up at about six o'clock feeling like an arthritic pretzel. I slapped my arms and legs until they were just drowsy, then did a U-turn, passing Deirdre's house. The Cadillac was gone and it was time for me to go to work.

As I drove around in cab forty-one I thought about the case, trying to figure out what the hell to do next. It bothered me that Deirdre was my client. And though I was glad to have avoided confronting my past, I was truly hurt that she had not recognized me. I didn't really have a self-image anymore so it was a small thing, like a BB in a can of paint, but it was in there and it was stirring things up. She was part of a past I had never expected to confront again—though God knows why I thought that. In a town this size you run into people you know every day. I never was very good at thinking things through.

But whatever I thought of Deirdre as a client, I had taken her case. I was supposed to solve it. And this disappearance *was* really odd, on the surface at least. Usually a person goes missing for some reason. There would be some clues. There didn't seem much to go on here. The guy's there one day, living in the big house with the pretty lady, the next he's gone. Then there was that odd burglary. Books? I would think about that one awhile—there were so many things they hadn't mentioned in my correspondence course.

I put in my night, dealing with the hookers, the out-of-town businessmen, the drunks, and the little old lady shoppers—especially one lady. We called her the bag lady, but she's not your usual bag lady. She's a little old lady the size of a corn fritter who stoops on her way to the cab because she's carrying stacks of cardboard boxes. She carries the boxes in her gnarled hands from an address in Browne's Addition, puts them into the cab, and delivers them all over the city. But she never seems to get rid of them. When she returns from an address she's still carrying boxes with her. Maybe they're new ones, but they look the same. I used to be really curious about her and what she was doing, what was in the boxes, and who she was taking them to. Then one day I found out. She opened the boxes and they were full of paper shopping bags, all of which had been used at least once. After that I didn't want to know who she was delivering them to, or why. There are a million stories in the city and they were all written by Rod Serling.

The next morning, feeling the effects of a lack of sleep, I wandered down to Mercer Manor, Inc., to talk to the manager and anyone else I could catch. The office was on West Third where the commercial district peters out into Browne's Addition and the freeway. It was a big office, recently built out of salmon-colored brick. It had a shake roof and a big wooden sign on top advertising *Mercer Manor* in fancy script. Like most classier real estate offices, there were no bulletin boards in the window advertising properties, just rust-colored curtains and a sign on the door that said: *Welcome to Mercer Manor. Tasteful Homes for People of Taste. Commercial Properties Available.*

I stepped from the overcast day into the oddly soothing fluorescent light of the office. The large room contained row upon row of simulated-walnut desks. There were a couple of lookers in the office, all nylons and earrings, and they examined me as I walked in. The polyester leisure suit crowd was making calls or talking to clients huddled respectfully at their desks. An older couple nearby seemed to be shocked at something and were talking together in hushed tones. Maybe they weren't getting a good enough market price for their house or maybe the salesman had told them an off-color joke.

One of the lookers approached me with a smile. I guess she knew that a lot of financially solid buyers dress as badly as I do. She was a shapely, auburn-haired girl in her mid-twenties, with a bob haircut, big brown eyes a little too made-up, a cute pointed nose, and lips that could have removed your tattoo. Her dress was a tight, lavender number that hugged her as she walked and reassured me I wasn't the only one in the world with questionable taste.

"Can I help you?" she asked when she was within reach.

"I'm looking for your manager, Mr. Baum," I told her.

"If this is about a house, perhaps I could help.

Bud is pretty busy."

"It's not about a house. I'm a detective looking into the disappearance of your boss."

I've always wanted to say that to someone.

"Well, actually Mr. Baum is my boss. The man who disappeared, Mr. Mercer, was an owner." She started away, then turned and said, "May I have your card?"

I patted my pockets. "Sorry, I'm fresh out. Maybe next time."

Bubbles looked disappointed, but she continued toward some back offices which were enclosed, but had windows so they could observe the rabble at the rows of desks. She was lovely going away.

I cooled my heels for ten minutes while she had a *tête-a-tête* with Bud. Eventually she stepped out of the door and signaled to me like a girl indicating it was okay to come and meet her folks now that they had cooled down from the initial shock of our engagement.

I strolled through the zoo as Bubbles held open the door to Baum's office. I could see him inside, standing expectantly beside his desk. He was in his middle forties, but he kept his graying-brown hair long, over his ears. Metal-rimmed glasses perched on his large nose. He was a handsome, "with it" guy who had a tan that made him look like he just returned from a week in Hawaii—and for all I knew, he had. He was tall and lean and fit. The most unhealthy looking things about him were his lime green leisure suit and white shoes. It's 1978, though, so he's in good company.

"Bud Baum," he said, smiling his best salesman smile and extending his hand. Bubbles peeked though the door at us once more before she closed it.

"I'm Scott Moody of Moody Investigations," I said. We shook hands.

"I understand you're here about Wendell." Baum sat, picked up a pencil from his desk, and played with it. I sat opposite him.

"I just want to know why he took off."

Baum laughed. "We'd all like to know." He held the pencil in his hands like he was about to break it. "I don't have a clue. As far as I knew, Wendell was happy. He had a beautiful wife, a good business. At first I thought he'd been kidnapped or maybe hurt in an accident. But then no note came and he hasn't turned up at the hospital or the morgue. I don't know. We had to hire two extra people to keep the business going. I've taken charge of the business while he's gone. We used to run it together."

"Someone gained, then," I said.

The constant smile disappeared. He looked like he'd just discovered a bug in his piña colada. "If you're here to cause trouble you won't get far," he said.

"I didn't mean anything by it," I lied. "I'm trying to find out if anything unusual was going on before Mercer disappeared. Did he have some home trouble, depressed at work, girlfriend—anything?"

"Nothing," he said.

"Anyone around here know Mr. Mercer better than you did? I hear you were sort of his right-hand man." I wondered what I could get out of this visit. It was my only lead at the moment. I was in over my head. Why the hell was I doing this? The only thing I knew anymore was how to drive cab. And actually I was only so-so at that.

"No one I can think of. I socialized a little with the Mercers. No one else spent much time with them. Mercer was pretty busy, put in fourteen-hour days usually. He had lunch with a few people, but that's about it. I frankly don't think you're going to find much here."

"I have to start somewhere. There's always a reason when someone disappears. They don't just *disappear*."

He frowned, then smiled. "Interesting logic," he said. "Anything more I can do for you?"

"I'd like to talk to some of your people. Perhaps do a few background checks, just on the outside chance someone here knew Mercer better than you think or knows something about why Mercer is missing."

Baum frowned again and poked his pencil at his lips, apparently deciding how to say something. He seemed to need a lot of emotional support from his writing instruments. "I know Deirdre's asking you to look into this, but I'll tell you, frankly, I don't want you bothering the sales staff. I'm sure that you're a fine young man trying to do your job, but I don't want you wandering around the office having conferences with my people. You won't find many of them in the office most days anyway. The only reason they're here now is that we have a meeting in five minutes.

"I'll tell you what I can do," Baum said, grinning now as though he were my best friend, "I can ask around myself. In fact, I can bring it up at the meeting this morning."

Oh, that'll be fine, I thought, *we'll get a hell of a lot of answers that way*, but I could see there was no point in pursuing it. He had one of these iron smiles that mean he's going to screw you and make you like it. If he had treated the police and the other detective this way, it was obvious why they hadn't made any progress. "All right," I replied. "I'll drop back in a few days to find out what you've learned. Then I'll follow up any leads." The smile faded. He didn't seem too interested in ever seeing me again. I punched the recorder and picked it up. I stood.

"Thanks a lot, Bud," I said and headed for the door.

"Anytime," he answered, meaning never. I walked out.

I strolled down the aisle between the desks. As I was nearing the front door, Bubbles caught up with me.

"Could I talk to you just for a moment?" She caught her breath as though she'd just run a mile instead of the short hop from her desk. She was even cuter when she was excited.

"What about?"

"Mr. Mercer. I just want you to know, a friend of mine used to go out with him. She doesn't work here anymore and I haven't seen her for awhile. I just always wondered if they didn't keep in contact, I mean, if he's still all right."

"Do you think . . . ?"

"Hey, I really can't talk here, not now. Can you meet me over at Perkins on Third in about half an hour?"

I thought about it, just for effect. "Yeah, I can do that. I'll be at the counter."

She hurried back to her desk and I walked out.

The Perkins she had mentioned was a franchise restaurant a few blocks away. It used to be a Smitty's some years before, but Perkins took it over. I parked outside as the car radio blared a news broadcast about the absent-minded bandit. The absent-minded bandit was a guy who had hit quite a few quick-stop markets during the past month or so. His peculiarity was that he often forgot what he was doing during a robbery. Once, he left a pair of gloves, and another time he forgot the money. When he came back fifteen minutes later to get the money, the police were nearing the store, and he barely escaped. This news story told of his most recent exploit in which he'd robbed a store just two hours before he came back to rob it again. His specialty was hitting a number of groceries in quick succession, then quitting for the day. Smart plan except for the idiosyncrasies.

I woke to a tapping on my window and I grabbed for my gun. Since I don't own a gun I came up with my finger pointing at Bubbles, the girl from the real estate office. I rolled the window down and watched her pout.

"I thought you were going to be at the counter," she said, obviously put out.

"Sorry, I didn't get much sleep yesterday and I must have dozed off. C'mon, I'll buy you a cup of coffee." I got out and followed her into the cafe. Following her was fun.

When we were settled into a booth and had coffee in front of us I asked her, "Okay, what do you know about Mercer? You think you know where he is?"

She was staring at me.

It was the nose thing again.

"You sure have a crooked nose," she said.

"Yeah. I was in Vietnam. I got it when a bunker collapsed. What's the deal with Mercer?"

"Your nose looks okay. You don't have to be sensitive about it."

I was about as sensitive as a bowl of farina. "I think you're cute too," I said, and smiled. What you don't have to do to get a little information.

She beamed at that one, shook her head to rearrange her hair, and said, "I'm not sure if this means anything at all. I just wouldn't want a friend of mine to get into trouble. I think she might know where he is."

"Who is she? By the way, who are you?"

"My name is Sheila Woo." I raised my eyebrows a little and she said, "I was married. My ex-husband is Chinese." I nodded and she continued. "The other girl is Julia Baldwin. She used to work at the office, not as a salesperson—she said she'd never do that—but as a secretary. She used to work directly for Wendell. She's a sort of hippie-type person—you know, against everything progressive and didn't want any development. She's a vegetarian, too. She lives in a house with a lot of other weird people."

"Doesn't sound like Wendell's type."

"She's not really. But she's very sexy and he liked that."

"How do you know?"

She looked irritated, turned out her pretty lower lip. "Not from personal experience," she said coldly. "I just know he flirted a lot when his wife wasn't around. I was still married most of the time we worked together and I never gave him any encouragement. With Julia it was different. She's the type who doesn't wear any underwear because she says it's too confining." She blushed and said, "They used to go out to lunch together, sometimes with other people, but a lot of times it was just the two of them. She quit work about a month before Mr.

Mercer disappeared."

"Where does she live?"

"Out toward Northtown—1313 Olympus. I wrote it down," she said, and handed me a card. "That's the last address we have on her."

"You don't seem to like her much. Why would you want to help her? For that matter, how are you helping her by turning her name over to me?"

"I didn't agree with her much, but she was my friend. I just thought that you wouldn't cause any trouble for her like the police would—if Mr. Mercer is with her. I never told the police about their friendship. Besides, if Mr. Mercer's found I don't want him to get into any more trouble than he has to. Mrs. Mercer shouldn't know about Julia by the way. Though, God knows, she's no angel either."

"What does that mean?"

She shrugged. "Nothing. I shouldn't talk about her."

"I'm not just gossiping. This is important."

"I don't really know very much. Mrs. Mercer worked at the office from time to time. She just seemed very friendly with a lot of the men."

"Nothing wrong with that."

"I guess not. I just think it was more than friendship sometimes."

"Bud?"

"I'm not going to say any more."

"So, do you want to see Mercer back?"

"Sure I do. He was easier to get along with than Bud. Bud is a real terror with his sales people. He's also a little predatory, if you know what I mean."

"Could you do me another favor?" I asked, studying the address of her friend. It was near Northtown, a shopping center a few miles from the center of the city. "Do you think you could get me a list of employees and their addresses? Just in case Julia doesn't have anything to do with this. Mercer's office is about my only lead at the moment."

"Bud wouldn't give you a list, huh?"

"Bud wouldn't give me the lint off his socks."

She giggled. She had a pretty smile that made her look about eighteen. She looked at me with happy brown eyes and said, "Bud didn't like you much. He isn't too enthused about anyone who would interfere with his authority. We used to hear all the time about how he came up the hard way and it was handed to Wendell on a silver platter."

"Can you get the list? Or will you?"

"Sure, I'll get you a list. How do I contact you?"

I ripped her card in half and wrote my number and name on it. "Try calling in the late afternoon, but if that's inconvenient just call anytime during the day. And one more thing. Could you also get me the names of any holding companies or partnerships that Bud or the Mercers are part of? I might have to do an asset search at some point. It'll be easier if I know the names to look for."

"Sure. There are only four or five—they're pretty commonly known at the office."

"Thanks, that'll help. Want any more coffee?"

"No. I might have a drink, though."

"I don't drink." That would discourage her. Boy, these young girls were getting to be murder.

"Oh. Well, I guess I'll see you later then, when you pick up the names. Let me know how everything goes."

"Okay." I paid the bill and we said our good-byes, then I headed home for some sleep.

I dreamed that I was in Vietnam dreaming that I was back home. I woke from the first dream to find myself in a bunker. I almost threw up. Then I was walking down the path to the latrine. On the way, I passed a bunch of soldiers who were questioning and torturing a villager at a leisurely pace. The villager was Wendell Mercer. Instead of arriving at the latrine, I found myself suddenly transported to a huge house at night. I was sitting in a living room that was dark except for the light from the fireplace. Deirdre Mercer was beside me. She leaned over to kiss me on the neck, and at the last moment I saw her vampire teeth. A conscious part of my mind wondered what the hell was the significance of this. I woke with a random thought echoing through my mind: *Are you all right?* it said. I almost answered, then remembered it was my unconscious, playing its old tricks.

I leaned on my elbow and lit a cigarette, pulling the smoke deep into my lungs. *I'll get you*, the voice in my head said, then faded. *I'll get you*, it echoed.

As on most mornings, I was in pain. It was the usual pain, pain that wandered all over my body—pain in my back, headaches, leg aches. Sometimes the pain was sharp, sometimes dull, sometimes excruciating. I was used to it. I had given up madness three months ago, and when you do that there's a price to be paid. The voices that had spoken to me during madness had had their ways of enforcing orders—through pain. When I gave it up, quit madness cold turkey and took up smoking in its place, the pain kicked in at a higher pitch. The best I could figure, it was a way for the voices to try to get me talking to them again. I'd had enough of that, and the pain seemed a better choice than going back to madness, back to taking their orders. These voices had turned me into a wandering zombie and now that I was out of it, feeling constant pain, dulled by Thorazine, I was relatively happy. The voices would come up again at moments of inattention—such as while waking up, or when I was very tired. Still, I had tuned them out for three months now. Like a nagging wife or an abusive parent, they droned on, kept trying to get me back in again, but I ignored them and kept going.

I switched on the radio, which buzzed and faded so that Billy Joel wavered in and out. My mind was like that cheap radio. Before my breakdown it had been a high-powered stereo with a good frequency response, with every thought distinct and clear and separate. Now it was a cheap portable, down to eight or ten thousand cycles with a few harmonics and noise thrown in for good measure. Not to mention that it was tuned to three stations at the same time. It was a good day for my appointment with the psychologist.

I looked at my watch. It was nearing four-thirty and I had to be at his office at five for a one-hour session before work. I dragged myself out of bed, trying to remember what had transpired that day. Oh yeah, earlier I had seen Bud Baum and Sheila Woo. Judging from the names, it was difficult to be sure I had not dreamed those encounters. What was I going to do next? I had no idea. I erased the tape from my mind except for *going to do next?* which echoed and reverberated.

My psychologist's office was in a run-down clinic near the cab lot on the north side. Dr. Houston shared a receptionist with a dentist and a veterinarian. This kind of cultural compromise was common in some of Spokane's less prosperous areas where businesses hung on by the slimmest of threads. It resulted in a waiting room decorated in mixed motifs—pictures of cats and dogs juxtaposed with flossing diagrams and sets of artificial teeth. On the psychologist's door a copy of the *Desiderata* clung to the wall.

When I arrived, Alma, his white-haired receptionist, was managing her switchboard and appointment calendar with equal incompetence. She had a small, birdlike face and nervous eyes that quivered behind those 1950s glasses that look like wings. As I walked up to the desk she glanced fearfully from my face to the ringing telephone. She was like that all the time, afraid that she would insult someone no matter what she did.

"Go ahead, answer the phone, Alma," I said as I approached the desk.

She smiled with relief and picked up the receiver.

A couple of kids waited with their mother— probably dental patients. A homely young woman held her cat. At the end of one of the couches a man tried to restrain a poodle that was showing an untoward interest in the cat.

Before Alma had cleared up her phone lines, Dr. Houston emerged from his office. He was escorting an obviously distraught young woman who was afflicted with near-terminal pallor and the greasies. Her long black hair hung in clumps on her faded, fraying sweater. She stared at Houston with her narrow-set black eyes as he told her, "Do the exercises I showed you and try to relax. Get an appointment for next week."

"Scott," Houston said when he saw me. "Come in, come in. Would you like a cup of coffee?"

"Thanks, it might help me to wake up." I followed him into the office and watched as he poured me a cup from his Mr. Coffee.

"Sugar, right?"

"Just a little," I said, then watched as he poured half the container into my cup. This was a ritual with us, and I wondered from time to time if it was intentional. He handed it to me and I sipped it, grimacing a little at the sweetness. Houston sat behind his desk and folded his hands.

He was dressed as usual in cord pants and hiking boots with a well-worn tweed sports jacket and a work shirt. He was in his late fifties. His face was cherubic and included a large bulbous nose that might have been caused by too much drink. He had lost most of his hair, and what remained was white like Alma's. He looked like Santa Claus, and for that reason he was the perfect therapist for me. I had always missed that old fellow.

Houston's office was the opposite of Nat Goodie's. It was crummy and small. There were boxes of folders and flyers all over the place—notices of retreats and seminars he was holding. A couple of ski boots loafed in the corner near an old sweater. The floor was littered with used Kleenex—the orange rinds of sorrow. His degrees and honors were nailed up on the dark wood paneled wall, all of them crooked and apparently randomly placed.

"Well, Scott, how are you today? How are things going?" His voice was gentle and deep and irritated the hell out of me.

"Pretty good. I have a couple of things bothering me."

"Only a couple? Sounds like you're making progress."

"I'm out of the hospital, if that's what you mean." I sipped the coffee again, then put it on the floor beside the chair where I would leave it. I looked out the window. The cars in the parking lot weren't doing anything.

"So, c'mon, Scott. You only get an hour every two weeks. Let's try to get something accomplished." Houston took a Kleenex from a box on his tired oak desk and wiped his nose.

"Well, it's about this case I'm on."

"Case?"

"Yeah, I guess I didn't tell you. I'm a private detective now. I got my license the other day."

He seemed mildly alarmed. "I didn't even know you were trying to get one."

"Well, I was and I did."

"You didn't have any trouble?"

"No. Mainly they decide based on references, and since I'm from Spokane, I have lots of relatives and old family friends. I know a couple of PIs—that helped."

"The city doesn't know you were in a mental hospital?"

"No. You planning on telling them?"

"No. That was out of state, and as far as I'm concerned you're as well as most people. I'm not sure, but this might be good for you. When did you get the idea you wanted to be a detective?"

"When I was in the hospital."

"When you weren't rational?"

"That's right. It was a fantasy of mine. It was during the time when I was talking to Humphrey Bogart a lot."

"During your hallucinatory states?"

"Yes. Mostly we were involved in the plot of *The Big Sleep*. The difference was that the story's villains were mostly administrators at the mental hospital."

He laughed. "So you want to be a knight?"

"A knight?"

"Yeah. You want to slay evil, rescue the fair damsel. Private investigators are all knights—at least that's our myth about them. Didn't you know?"

"Not really. I suppose I wanted to be a hero. At the time, actually, I was feeling very paranoid and assumed I would be killed in some government plot."

"Why didn't it wear off like the rest of the fantasy?"

"I don't know. It just didn't. Even when I got well it's what I wanted to do."

"You're not planning to get a gun, are you?" he said, suddenly.

"No, I don't need a gun."

"I thought detectives aways had guns."

"No, I don't think so."

"So you're not considering getting one?"

"No."

He seemed satisfied enough with my answers to move on to the next topic, but I was a little irritated. It was a good thing I didn't have a gun.

"Scott, I'd like a little more information about your episode. I just received the hospital records, and it seems that it was a little more severe than you've led me to believe."

"I don't really want to talk about that."

"You pretty much have to. It's a condition of your release from the hospital."

"What do you want to know? Why I went crazy?"

"Not exactly a technical term."

"It is to me. Also bananas, wacko, goofy, and loony."

"How did your illness start?"

"At first I was only mad in the philosophical sense."

"Philosophical?"

"Yeah. I started believing in life after death."

"A lot of people believe in that."

"They're crazy, believe me."

"How did that lead to madness?"

"These people I met told me I could talk to the dead. Then they seemed to back it up by doing it. They used a Ouija board to contact them."

"That's just a parlor game."

"Not if you're crazy enough. Some people think you can talk to the dead that way."

"Well, if you contacted the dead, who did you contact?"

"It's a funny thing. When someone tells you they can contact the dead you react like you do sometimes when you look at a phone book in a strange town. You think, 'Who do I know here?' That's what I did. I thought, 'Who do I know who's dead?' I thought about an old friend of mine, a guy who died in Vietnam. But as it turned out, I didn't contact him—not at first, anyway."

"Who did you contact?"

"My mother. At the time I thought it was my mother."

"We talked about her in an earlier session, didn't we? You said she died when you were little."

"She died when I was four. It had been so long that I had forgotten about her when I thought about who did I know who was dead. But she answered instead—or, as I said, I thought it was her. Turned out to be an impostor."

"This must have affected you deeply."

"Your mom's been dead for nearly thirty years and suddenly you think you're talking to her— yeah, it affected me. I cried a lot. It seems stupid now, but I guess I so desperately wanted her alive that I conjured her up." I patted my pockets looking for a cigarette. When I talked about this stuff, I needed a little more support. Since I didn't carry cigarettes with me, I wasn't going to get any.

"You don't think it was really your mother?"

"Not any more. It took a lot of time to convince me. I went mad. I got divorced, I lost everything I owned. I got thrown in jail."

"Why'd you get thrown in jail?"

"I was crazy."

"*Why* did you get thrown in jail?"

"I walked into a house that wasn't mine."

"Why'd you do that?"

"My mother told me it was my house—that she was giving it to me."

"Now *that* is *bananas*," Houston said.

He wanted to make me laugh and I laughed, but it was a gallows laugh. It was the kind of laugh that punctured a balloon full of tragedy. I ran my hand through my hair. "I still listened to her, even after that. Eventually, I had to let her die all over again. And my friend too. I couldn't live if they stayed alive inside me. After I had suffered for a very long time, I knew, finally, that they were impostors."

"Why did you want to contact your friend? It seems kind of crazy on the face of it—thinking you could contact the dead."

"Hey, it's the seventies. Anything is possible."

"But why this particular friend?"

"I missed him. I felt bad about his death. I felt guilty."

"Why did you feel guilty? Did you have something to do with his death?" Houston lit a cigarette. I still wanted a cigarette, but he would not be able to help me. He smoked Kools.

"No, of course not. He died in Vietnam."

"So why did you feel guilty?"

"You don't get anything, do you? You weren't in

the service, were you?" I liked Houston, but he was pissing me off.

"No, I don't get it. I wasn't in the service. I'll get it if you explain it to me. Why do you feel guilty?" He exhaled the foul Kool smoke. I detected a hint of menthol in the air.

"Because I went to Vietnam too."

"I know that. What's that got to do with it?"

"I came back and he didn't."

"That's why you're guilty?"

"Yes. That's why we're all guilty. All of us who went and didn't die. We were supposed to."

"Supposed to die?"

"Yeah. That was the deal. That's what we were sent there to do. We weren't supposed to come back. But some of us didn't cooperate."

"So you felt as if the people at home had sent you there to die?"

"Sure seemed like it to me." It was a stupid point of view, but I was on the verge of sobbing anyway.

"But your friend did die. He performed the sacrifice, not you, so you felt guilty."

I gasped a little as I held back my sobs. "Can I have one of your cigarettes?"

He handed me one of the Kools and I lit it. Jesus, I hated the taste. "So you were guilty—you sought out your dead friend and you ended up hearing voices."

"Yeah."

"But you got your control back."

"Yeah."

"Part of your control is being angry, isn't it?"

"Angry as hell."

"You ever feel you'll lose control?"

"Sometimes. I don't think I'd lose it for long. But who knows. My subconscious is a little more active than most. Generally, people experience their subconscious very little—in dreams, in little incidents. Like when you're holding buttered toast, lose attention and your hand seems to act on its own, throws the toast butter-down on the floor. But my subconscious is like King Kong. It *really* wants to run things. It tries hard to get control. After all, it was in charge once. So far, I'm staying ahead of it."

But just barely.

Houston extinguished his cigarette in the ashtray. "Do you mind coming back to the present?"

"Happily." If happily was ever the right word for my experience.

"This new job, this job where you don't need a gun, how do you like it so far?" he asked. "You making any money?"

"Some. The money's not the issue though. I'm still working as a cab driver, so I'll survive. It's the woman."

"What woman?"

"One involved in the case. Her husband is missing. Turns out she's a girl I went to college with. We used to go steady back when that was the word for it."

"Have you talked about the old times?" He picked up a pipe I had never seen him smoke and stuck it into his mouth, unlit. I had finally had enough of the Kool and I crushed it, perhaps a little cruelly, in the ashtray.

"She didn't recognize me—or didn't admit that she did. I look a little different these days and she was pretty drunk when we met—in the middle of the day."

"What's bothering you about this?"

"I don't know exactly. It's just that she affected me in some way. I haven't cared one way or the other about women since I got out of the hospital. I can't afford to, you know. . ."

"Yeah, we talked about this. You're afraid you won't be able to perform—sexually."

"You know, I don't like to talk about this."

"I know."

"I just hate women or ignore them. It's easier."

"I understand. But this woman you can't ignore."

"Yeah. For some reason she's on my mind. I'm sad about her life. I'm sad about my life. I'm sad that we've lost the past—our youth. She's gotten to me. I preferred it when no one got in."

"It's a good sign, Scott. You're starting to feel again."

"I don't want to feel again—other than maybe a little pissed off."

"What are you going to do?"

"Ignore my feelings. It's what I'm good at."

"Well, we'll see what happens. I'll be interested to know."

"I'll be observing it myself," I said, imitating his attitude. "Though I don't really give a damn."

"That your only problem?"

I looked at the floor. "Other than that, I miss my daughter."

"How old is she now?"

"Four. Just four."

"You still don't feel like seeing her?"

"Not for awhile. I'm not ready yet."

"I hope that changes soon. She seems awfully damned important to you for you to go on ignoring her."

"I just can't face her after what's happened. I'm ashamed to tell her that I'm the father she's stuck with."

"You were a little sick for awhile. It's okay to be

sick."

"Not like that, not crazy."

"Take your time, but think about her. She hasn't seen you in how long now?"

"Three months." I wept quietly and added to the Kleenex on the floor.

CHAPTER THREE

I got to work at six that evening and took out a rattletrap with a Hurst floor shift and back doors that wouldn't open from the inside. It was one cab the fares wouldn't run out on.

I cruised around town for a while, ferrying business people back and forth. It was a Friday, and fairly busy. Then I got Ralph the Redundant in the car. Ralph was a wizened, fifty-year-old alcoholic. He always wore a dirty trench coat and a brown fedora and he repeated the same things every time you picked him up, drunk and sloppy from a downtown gin mill. He would get into the car and say, "First, I want to apologize. I'm not going a long way. I'm not going to the airport or anything. I'm just going a short way," and then he would give the address of his apartment house on West Riverside. On the way there he would say, "I know what you cabbies go through. My brother-in-law was a cabbie. He drove for Yellow Cab for thirty years. Had to give it up because of hemorrhoids. Boy, was he sore!" and then he would cackle like hell. Same words every time. I kicked him out of the cab at his apartment, accepted a nickel tip, and went on my way.

It was two hours before I got a run up north. When I had taken my fare to his address I called in for a bathroom stop, but instead drove around to 1313 Olympus, the address Sheila Woo had given me for her former co-worker.

The house was old and run-down. Weeds and dry grass grew knee deep in the yard, and a few old trucks and cars loafed on various dead patches of ground, waiting for someone to cannibalize them. The house was covered by composition shakes, a dark green originally, but now most had faded to about the shade of Bud Baum's suit. The shake roof was smothered in moss and decay.

I didn't have much time so I left the cab running, trotted up onto the porch and knocked on the time-worn white door.

A few seconds later the door jerked open with a squawk, as though it had imploded from a sudden vacuum inside the house. A fat, bearded man in his late thirties stood in the doorway, his hand still gripping the doorknob. Most of the hair on his head was gone. A mustache and wire-rimmed glasses decorated his chubby face. His chest and shoulders and stomach, covered by a worn T-shirt, reminded me of those smiling statues of Buddha as a fat guy.

"Yeah?" he said. It wasn't so much a question as a challenge.

"Is Julia around?"

"Who wants her?"

"Scott." I hoped just a first name would be ambiguous enough that she might assume I was a long-lost friend.

"Okay." He left the door without inviting me in and a moment later a young woman came out. I could see what Wendell Mercer might have seen in her. Her face was dark, with large brown eyes and full, wide lips. It was one of those perfect, sculptured faces of women at art shows—in the company of equally perfect male specimens. She was a woman who exuded something special: intelligence, taste, sensuality. Her long, dark-brown hair draped her back and hips. She wore a peasant blouse with a Danskin underneath, jeans, and moccasins.

"I don't know you," she said the moment she appeared.

"You don't," I affirmed. "We have a friend in common."

"Oh, who?" She didn't seem truly curious, more suspicious and aloof. That's another thing she had in common with other beautiful women—she intimidated the hell out of me.

"Wendell Mercer."

I could have sworn she blushed, and that interested me.

"He used to be my boss. That's all I know about him. I haven't worked for him for months."

"You haven't seen him since then?"

"No, why? What's this all about?" It was a natural question, but her voice seemed a trifle nervous to me.

"He's missing, or haven't you heard? No one knows where he is. I heard you two were pretty close and I wondered if he had contacted you."

She laughed derisively. "We weren't close. I went out to lunch with him, but that's not close. He was my boss. He was nice, but I'm not much interested in people who spend their lives in pursuit of money. I just think you'll have to ask someone else." She started to close the door and I stuck my foot into the opening. That was a mistake, because then she slammed it on my toes. It hurt like hell.

"Ow, Christ!" I yelped. I hopped around a little on the porch and she opened the door again, to watch, I guess.

"What's going on here?" a man's voice asked from the room next to the hallway. He appeared suddenly, the big, heavyset fellow, with a tall, skinny guy behind him. The new one looked a little like James Taylor, but his features were thinner, harder, more cruel. His hair was thinning and he also had a mustache.

"Is this guy bugging you?" the heavy guy asked Julia, turning a scowling eye toward me.

"He's asking a lot of questions, Chicken Man. I think he's a cop or something and I don't want to talk to him." The door was wide open now, but as I stood there on the porch on one foot, massaging my toes, I'd have preferred it be closed.

"He's no cop," said Chicken Man. "He's driving that cab. What the hell do you want with my friend, fella?"

"Just a few questions, that's all. No harm, really." I was on two feet now, but gingerly.

"Buddy, you'd better split before Chicken Man comes down on you," said the skinny guy.

"He'll go, all right," said Chicken Man. "I'll help him," and he grabbed me by the neck and belt and hoisted me like a sack of grain. I'm six feet and weigh 180, but the way the guy handled me I could have been an air mattress. He catapulted me into a bunch of weeds and grass that were wet from the April rain. I always hate to end a visit like that.

I lay there for a moment catching my breath and overcoming a pain in my back. Then I rose, wet and bruised, and hobbled toward the cab.

"Stay the hell away from here, creep," said Chicken Man. "I can do worse when I get really pissed off." The group watched as I drove away.

When I went back on shift I got a chewing-out from the dispatcher because he had a call for my cab while I was being beaten up. He put me on a cab stand downtown and I spent most of the night being ignored.

The next morning when I got off I was still sore as hell and bore a grudge against the people at 1313 Olympus. I went to Casey's, an all-night restaurant on Monroe Street, for breakfast and brooding. My pride was hurt by my treatment and so was my back. It made me think about pursuing the fat guy and Baby James even though I had no reason to connect them with Mercer. I thought about turning them in to the police, but I didn't think the authorities would pay much attention to my complaint.

Sally, the chubby, middle-aged waitress who served me most mornings at Casey's, took my order for bacon and eggs and coffee.

"Ovaries?" she asked.

"Huh? What?"

"Over easy?" she repeated.

"Oh. Yeah." Boy, what working nights and getting beat up won't do for your hearing.

The first thing after breakfast I called the detective who had worked this case before me. He was a nice guy, but he told me in no uncertain terms that he wasn't happy to have been replaced. He said he had done a very thorough search. He had looked through Wendell's papers for clues. He had called the Mercers' travel agent. He had checked with their doctor, pharmacy, and hospital for any medical activity since his disappearance. He also listed a number of other records he had used to pursue his quarry. Most of his investigative techniques were new to me, but I tried to sound as though I approved and understood them all. He finished our conversation with a cryptic comment: "I got to tell you, Moody, I wonder if this guy's still alive."

"What does that mean?"

"Just a hunch. Either he's dead or he's not doing any transactions anywhere under his own name—like he joined witness protection or something. You know, people generally turn up. They get jobs, they buy prescriptions—they generate a paper trail. I haven't seen a sign of a paper trail. One way or another, he's become a ghost."

I drove the Pinto downtown and parked on Sprague. I was following a hunch I had been thinking about since my beating the night before. I drifted down the street until I came to a bookstore. I went in and talked to the guy at the counter, showing him the picture of Wendell Mercer. I tried at several bookstores with no success until I visited Gandalf's Books on West Sprague. Gandalf's was large for a used bookstore, with a main floor and a mezzanine covered with the wood flooring you used to see in general stores, gray and rough, the kind you sweep with a broom and cleaning compound. The shelves were stacked high with first editions, occult crap, and memorabilia of the 1950s and 1960s. They also had a large collection of underground comics and some general-interest paperbacks for the uninitiated browser. It was the kind of place where employees, and most of the people shopping there, behaved as though they were involved in something very grave and important. You could be there an hour and the clerk wouldn't look at you unless he heard the rustle of green and the slap of a book on the counter.

I walked up to the young man sitting at the cash register reading *Finnegans Wake*. He didn't hear the rustle of money or the thump of a book, so he didn't look up. He was in his twenties, his hair was shaggy brown, and his beard was peach fuzz.

"Excuse me," I said.

He looked over his rimless glasses, an existential question posed by his blue eyes.

"I'm looking for someone," I said.

"This is a bookstore," he replied.

"I'm looking for someone in a bookstore," I said. I put the pictures of Wendell on the counter before him. "I just wondered if you've ever seen this man in the store."

"Are you with the police or something?" he asked, still aloof. It's 1978 and young people don't like the police. It's like they figure drug dealers and rock stars are the only ones with moral values.

"I'm a private detective." I pulled out my wallet and showed him my I.D.

"He owes money or something?"

"He's missing. His wife wants to know where he is."

"Oh." He warmed up about as much as liquid nitrogen, but he studied the pictures, which I took to be a good sign.

"I don't know for sure," he said after a minute. "He looks vaguely familiar."

"He could look different now, longer hair, beard," I coached.

"No, I don't think that's it. I think I've seen him, I just can't put him into context. Oh, wait a minute. This guy is interested in underground art and comics."

"Huh?"

He gave me a supercilious look and pointed toward a stack of comics and posters. "People collect these," he said. "They become valuable over time— the comics, not the people."

"Oh, yeah." I was about as interested in underground comics as the artists themselves, now that they had gone to work for Disney or Hanna Barbera, but I tried to feign interest as I glanced at a stack of *Furry Freak Brothers* and *Zap Comix*. "Nice selection. Any particular time of the week or day he comes in? I'd like to speak to him."

"No particular day of the week. He seems to favor evenings, though."

That figured.

I glanced out the window and saw a cab stand across the street at a run-down hotel. "Thanks for your time," I said and left. Maybe I wouldn't have to bother the people at 1313 Olympus again, or rather, they wouldn't have to bother me. This was pretty cool. I had been a detective for only a few days and already I knew something no one else seemed to know with certainty—Wendell Mercer was still alive.

I went home and slept, drifting off during a Donahue discussion of the merits of clipping manufacturers' coupons to supplement the food budget. I'm surprised I didn't have nightmares about it.

I woke to a phone ringing. At first I thought it was the clock, then after I had crushed that with my hand I decided it was the doorbell, which I don't have. By the time I figured out that it was the phone, Sheila had been ringing for more than a minute and was impatient.

"Why didn't you answer sooner?" she said. I could hear the music of Al Stewart in the background, and I imagined her sitting on a carpet surrounded by a cloud of incense, and smoking a joint. I further imagined that she was wearing a nightgown with nothing underneath.

"I'm a night worker," I told her. "I try to sleep sometimes."

"Oh. I guess your work would be somewhat nocturnal. I never thought about it really."

I didn't bother clarifying. I didn't mind if she went a little longer thinking I wasn't scum. At least not taxi-driving scum. "What do you want?" I asked.

"I have the list for you. You wanted the list of employees and the names of Mercer's holding companies. I got the information for you."

"Oh. Okay. Why don't we meet in the next couple of days and I'll get it from you." I looked at my watch. It was two o'clock. I wondered where she could be with music like that in the background. I didn't give a damn about the list anymore. With a little luck I could locate Wendell through the bookstore. "How about on Monday at about five at Perkins? Today *is* Friday, isn't it?"

"Today is *Saturday*," she said with some exasperation.

"Oh." No wonder. She was at home. "Well, is Monday okay?"

"I guess so. I was thinking this weekend would be better—at my place. I'm kind of afraid of being seen with you near work. Bud doesn't approve of you."

"I'm working tonight. How about tomorrow?"

"Okay. Make it sometime in the late afternoon. Would you like something to eat? I could fix dinner."

I was silent so long she said, "Hello? Hello? Are you still there?"

"Yeah," I said finally. "I could eat." I accepted out of politeness, which was completely out of character. She gave me her address and I wrote it on my notepad in Sanskrit. Then I passed out again until six. I had to scramble to get to work.

"You're becoming unreliable, Moody," said the dispatcher as I signed out the worst cab on the lot. "You'd better watch it."

"Sure," I told him. I wasn't too worried. The last time they had fired a driver it was because he had murdered a passenger. And they did that for public relations purposes.

I drove on five cylinders and signed in on the stand by the Oasis Rooms, the hotel across from Gandalf's. The dispatcher said, "Where?" when I told him, then gave me a laconic "Okay," which spoke volumes. He wasn't going to give me the satisfaction of asking why I had chosen a dead stand. I guess when you work with enough crazy people you just don't want to know anymore.

I sat there for an hour, watching a steady stream of aging hippies, college professors, and neophyte intellectuals flow into and out of Gandalf's. I didn't see anyone resembling Wendell. This method of finding him might work, but it would take time.

About seven-thirty the back door of my cab opened and a guy got in. I glanced back, then I turned around and looked. He was a husky man, construction worker or carpenter type, wearing a workshirt, jeans, make-up, and a woman's wig.

"Hey, buddy," he said, "Take me to the Blue Bull." He was soused.

"Yeah, sure," I answered. I didn't want to ask why the make-up and wig. I dropped him off at the Blue Bull and returned to the cab stand. When I signed in, the dispatcher said, "You must be independently wealthy," and left it at that.

I sat at the cab stand for a while before I noticed there was a new addition at Gandalf's. It was Julia Baldwin. She was looking through the comic books. What was with these people and comic books? Of course it helped if you were stoned, and I hadn't been stoned for a long time.

Was she buying for Wendell? I thought about following her, but I knew where she would go and there I would have to contend with Baby James and Chicken Man. I'd stick it out at Gandalf's a few more nights to see if Mercer showed up. Goodie hadn't put a time limit on this, and I wanted to keep my limbs intact.

Julia Baldwin left after half an hour or so, not giving me so much as a glance, and got into an old Ford pickup I had seen parked in the yard of 1313 Olympus. Funny, I'd thought it was defunct. When she roared out of sight I asked the dispatcher if I could move off the stand and try somewhere else.

He said, "Please do."

I woke the next afternoon with a hell of a headache. I took half a bottle of Excedrin and watched an Abbott and Costello movie, but I knew nothing would help. This was part of the price of giving up conversations with my voices. It was a kind of punishment from the subconscious and I was used to it. When I went over to Sheila's the headache was still with me and I was in no mood to be polite. Then Sheila answered the door wearing a long dress and no underwear and that just made my mood worse. The smell of incense drifted out of her apartment.

"Hi, Scott," she said, jiggling a little. "Come in."

"I don't think I'll be able to stay for dinner," I told her, trying to keep my eyes off her breasts and the soft skin of her neck. "I'm not feeling too well."

"Oh, really?" She seemed disappointed and slouched in the doorway like a petulant child. A very sexy petulant child.

"Yes. I'd like to pick up the list, then I think I'm going home to bed."

She walked into the apartment and her voice drifted back to me. "I wish you could stay. I've prepared a delicious paella."

Now that I was in the hallway I could smell it.

"Yeah, I'm sorry, but that's the way I feel." I looked into her lair. The stereo was blaring *Abba* and there were place settings at a small table in the middle of the room. The table was covered with an oriental silk and decorated with candles. I felt bad about disappointing her, but I didn't want any part of that scene. Only a couple of years ago you couldn't have dragged me away from it.

She returned from the back room carrying two sheets of white paper with names and addresses on them. "This is a list of all the employees, including the other offices. I've checked the ones that work out of the main office."

I glanced at the sheet while she rubbed my shoulder.

"Are you sure you can't stay? I could give you a massage."

A rush of emotion passed through me. Excitement, disappointment, sorrow. I was probably blushing, but no one could have made me admit it. "No, I really can't, thanks. Why is this name crossed out?"

She looked at the list without moving her hand. It was burning a spot on my shoulder. Later I would have to use Solarcaine to treat it.

"Former employee. I knew him. He was a good guy. He couldn't have had anything to do with this."

"What's his name?"

"Pat . . . Patrick. I forget his last name."

I wrote it down in the margin. "Okay. This is fine. I'll see you later." I turned to go and her hand slipped from my shoulder.

"Have you learned anything yet about Wendell, I mean, Mr. Mercer?"

"Not much."

"Did you talk to Julia?"

"For a few minutes. She was discouraging. I doubt she knows anything."

"Oh." She seemed disappointed. "You'll let me know what you find out though, won't you?"

"Sure."

"And I'll see you later?" The question was punctuated by a meaningful and sensuous look.

"Sure," I told her, eloquent as always. "Bye."

I hot-footed it to my car and drove away. When I got home my phone was ringing. At first I thought the ringing was in my head, but it was merely being amplified by the throbbing of my headache.

When I finally answered I heard a woman's voice, vaguely familiar.

"Is Mr. Moody in?" it asked.

"No, he's not," I said.

"Scott? I can recognize your voice, you know," Deirdre said.

"How? You couldn't recognize me at all the other day." I was sounding brave and indifferent, but I wasn't feeling it.

"I knew who you were. It took a few minutes, but I knew."

"You could have fooled me."

"I'll be honest, Scott, I didn't like you. I didn't like your manner. I didn't even like your clothes."

"I'm not a snappy dresser anymore."

"You're not a snappy conversationalist either, Scott. What happened to you? Where have you been? When I tried to get your phone number, they said it was a new service. Have you been out of town?"

She paused, evidently waiting for me to add some information, but I stayed silent. I certainly wasn't going to tell her that I had only recently been able to afford a deposit toward getting a phone installed. We waited. I didn't know what to say to her. Things had changed so much. I had changed. I didn't want her to know that I had thrown my life onto the garbage heap. I didn't want her to think of me as one of those bums sitting on the curb waiting for the garbage truck to pick them up.

"I want to see you," she said finally.

"Why?"

"I want to see you."

"I don't know if that's a good idea."

"I'm your client. You'd better see me." The voice was hard and I didn't like it. "I don't think you should be on this case," she added.

"Why not?"

"That's what I need to talk to you about—among other things."

I looked down at my pack of cigarettes. I reached for one and held it between my fingers. "When?" I asked.

"Right away."

"I'll be over." I hung up. This was a hell of a situation. Deirdre Mercer was ordering me around and I had to take it. I lit the cigarette. She was giving me bad habits too.

When I got there every light in the house was lit. I could see Deirdre through the leaded-glass windows, pacing back and forth with a wine glass in her hand. She was holding it when she answered the door.

She smiled. "It's good to see you again," she said. "Really nice."

I was frowning. More of a grimace really. "Yeah."

"Come on in," she said, a smile lingering.

She was different than she had been on my first visit. She was soft and sensual, as she had been when we dated. It made me long for those old days, when we were kids with the softest of arteries.

"Would you like a drink?" she asked as I followed her into that expansive living room. I could smell the perfume. I tried to avoid looking at her body under the slinky dress.

"I'll have a little of your wine, I guess." I walked around the room like a cat in new surroundings. I refrained from howling, though.

She poured the wine and handed it to me. I tasted it and glanced at the bottle sitting on the bar. It was a *Pouilly Fuissé*—a little better than I usually drank. I think my last wine was a nice little Mad Dog 20-20. I hadn't had much of anything to drink since my release from the hospital. The doctor at my exit interview had warned me about drinking. The wine caressed my taste buds and told me stories on the way down. I let the wine talk but resisted talking back.

"Can I ask you something?" she said, adjusting

her dress as she settled into an armchair. I found a safe spot by the fireplace.

"Sure. Shoot." It was going to be the nose thing again.

"What happened to your nose? You're still good-looking, but it looks like you had an accident."

"That happened a few years after I left school," I told her. "I got hit by a baseball when I was in the Army."

She laughed. "That sounds like bullshit, Scott."

"It is," I said, "but I don't want to tell you what really happened."

She shrugged her beautiful shoulders. "Okay."

I swallowed a little of the wine and it told me another tale. It was a good one. I laughed at it. The doctor at the hospital had probably been right about drinking being bad for me.

"What?" asked Deirdre.

"Nothing. I just feel a little giddy. This is good wine. I can't have a second glass."

"You haven't changed much," she said. "You're as strange as ever." She seemed to be avoiding the point of this conversation.

"You wanted to talk to me about the case."

"I don't want to rush it," she replied, always in control. "The last I heard, you were studying to be a journalist. How did you become a private detective?"

"Like other people," I said. "I trained for it." Not very much, but I trained for it.

"Are you good at it?" She shifted her weight and lit a Salem. Suddenly I wanted a cigarette and for once I was prepared. I had stuck one into my jacket pocket. I took it out and lit it with my red Bic lighter. I preferred blue Bic lighters, but they had been out last time I was buying.

"I don't know whether I'm good at it or not, yet. This is my first case."

"That's too bad," she said. "Because I don't want you to work on this. I don't want to employ you on this case."

"I have clients," I told her. "Not employers."

"Pretty thin distinction."

"I go for thin distinctions."

"In any event, I want you to stop working. I thought I'd tell you before I told Nat Goodie."

"I want this case, Deirdre. I'm not going to screw it up." There was a begging tone in my voice that did not appeal to me.

"I don't think you're going to do anything wrong. That's a silly notion. I just don't want someone I know involved in this." There was clearly something else she wasn't saying, but I would never get it out of her.

"Well, it's a moot point anyway," I told her politely, "since I think I've found him."

She leaned forward. "You have?"

"I know where he is. I don't know the rest of the story, but I know where he is."

"Why haven't you brought him to me?"

"Is that what you want—him delivered to your door?"

"Yes."

"I'll bring him, but it'll be a while."

"I thought you knew where he was."

"I have a rough idea. It's a matter of separating him from his friends, and that will take a few days the way I have it planned. If it doesn't work, then I'll just call the police and have him rounded up."

"I'd rather do it in a quiet way. I don't want reporters in on this."

"Then I can do it in the next two weeks." I hoped.

"Would you turn this information over to another investigator?"

"Not without a fist fight." I'd lose, but I'd fight.

"Then I guess you'll do it," she said glumly, "but I warned you." She rose from her chair and came toward me. She took the wine glass out of my hand and put it on the mantel beside an ebony Buddha.

"Nice to see you again," she said, leaning forward and kissing me on the lips. I thought of pulling back, but I didn't. This was quintessential Deirdre. She appeared to be acting spontaneously, but you had the feeling she'd been planning it all along. She always organized, then attacked and got what she wanted. Years ago it was another man—boy—she wanted. After she was rid of me she got him. I suspected at the time it was my atheism that caused me to get the boot. It just didn't fit into her universe. "You'll do well in this world," she told me once, "but not in the next." So far I hadn't done all that well in this one. Too bad she hadn't met me when I was mad, during my religious phase. Of course, it only lasted until I got thrown into the mental hospital. I had sort of given up religion since then. It's a hazardous luxury for a psychotic.

She had one of her arms on my neck, the other resting inside my jacket. This felt too good, and when she had finished kissing me I drew back a little to relieve the pressure. My face was about five inches from hers. Her face had not changed much over the years. The skin was perfect—white and smooth, except for the little mole above her lip that I could feel when I kissed her. Her brown eyes were clear. Her eyebrows were thin and dark, giving her an elegant look but belying the blond of her hair. Her lips at this distance attracted me like the pull of a magnet, but, like the Enterprise caught in a tractor beam, I resisted.

"I've got to go," I said.

"Now?"

"Yes." I had nowhere to go and nothing to do.

"When will I see you again?" She was her old soft self now.

"When I have some information or when I deliver him."

"I'm going to divorce him, you know."

"Sounds like a good idea to me." Just keep me the hell out of it. I moved to the door. She followed "I'll see you later," I said. I closed the door behind me and started down the stairs in the darkness.

Out of that darkness someone punched me in the mouth. It was so surprising that I just stood there a moment, numb in the jaw. I waited politely while he moved around behind me, grabbed me by the throat, and started punching my kidneys out. I tried to break free, but his chokehold threatened to strangle me and his early blows knocked out my breath, immobilizing me. I couldn't help noticing that he had bad breath. Finally I wore the guy out and he took off after giving me one more blow, a shattering left to my side. Slowly, like a sawed-off Sequoia, I toppled, a dead weight, toward some shrubbery. "Sonofabitch," I mumbled.

I hit gently, bouncing on the low evergreen shrubs and rolling as the plants' resilience tried to throw me aside. I tumbled out onto the lawn, moaning and holding my stomach and back. I thought maybe I would just stay there awhile. No use rushing things.

Then the porch light came on and Deirdre was standing there looking around. "Scott?" she said. "Who's out there? Scott!"

I didn't make any reply. I thought moaning was

eloquent enough. Then she was beside me, holding my shoulders while I held my stomach.

"Scott, what happened? Are you all right?"

"Someone jumped me," I thought I said, but I must have just imagined that I said it, I must have been thinking it instead, because she didn't seem to hear me. She tried helping me to my feet, but at first I couldn't go anywhere. I couldn't see why she was in such a hurry to get me ambulatory again. I felt fine right where I was, but I wasn't in any shape to argue, and on the third try I was moving, like a hobbled horse, toward the front door. The steps were hard to climb and I yelled a little, but not enough that Deirdre had to slap me or anything. She led me to the back room, probably a guest bedroom, and helped me lie down on a bed about the size of the Astrodome.

I didn't argue when she began removing my clothes. I yelped a little, but I didn't argue. She had trouble with a sneaker because the laces had been too short to tie in a bow and had been formed into a mangled knot. She finally pulled it off without untying it and pinched my instep. I yelped again. I was sounding more like a Dachshund caught in a door than a man. Then I was on satin sheets, feeling a chill. I heard Deirdre making a phone call. I couldn't think of anything else I wanted to do, like roller skate or ride Brahma bulls, so I went to sleep, if you could call coma a kind of sleep.

Some big guy was beating on me, beating the hell out of my nose. I was on a pool table and he was taking the cue to me. Then I was floating, rising, like coming up from the bottom of a swimming pool. I floated at the edge of a clearing, and now I was a child watching deer at a salt lick. There had been a time like that in my childhood, and it seemed natural to be there instead of in bed or on a pool table. I lay there feeling the cool dampness of the earth and delighting in the graceful movements of the deer, until someone turned me over. I wasn't in the forest anymore. I was in Deirdre's house. I was being examined by an elderly doctor, and I caught glimpses of him as I moved between consciousness and sleep. After probing and prodding me for awhile, he left, and I guess they decided to leave me where I was. That was just fine with me. I slept a rare sleep, with no dreams.

I rolled over at dawn, stretching an arm and feeling a lovely soft hip beneath my hand. That was odd, but not unpleasant. Then she moved and I wasn't fully awake and I wasn't asleep and I wasn't able to resist or worry about the outcome. I wasn't sure at first, but then I knew I would be able to complete the lovemaking and I began to see images of depths and tunnels and whirlpools as she moved on top of me. The warmth was so new to me, I knew afterward I would be changed, no longer as afraid. She handled everything and I felt a need to touch her and my hands held the pendulous weight of her breasts and touched her hips and thighs and feet. I hugged her to me and amid the wetness and warmth and the softness of her hair on my shoulder and the touch of her cheek, I slept again.

When I woke I reached over and felt the inside of her thigh, her hair, her hip bones. I opened my eyes and Deirdre was watching me, her brown eyes clear and bright, not affected by sleep. Her blond hair lay in attractive disarray on her pillow.

"I've wanted to do that again for a long time," she said quietly. "I'm glad you were able to stay."

I didn't bother to protest that I had stayed because of the bogeyman with halitosis. I closed my eyes. I wasn't sure I could handle this closeness in the daylight, or face her with the truth about myself. She moved nearer and embraced me. Though I didn't participate, I didn't move away.

"I haven't made love with anyone for a very long time," I said finally, my voice cracking with hoarseness. I could still feel the distant ache of my body in the places I had been hit. I didn't want to move ever again. I wanted to stay in this bed until I was a very old man and pass away quietly in my sleep.

"That surprises me," she said. "You're such a nice-looking guy. You should have lots of girlfiends. Why would a guy like you go so long without a relationship?"

I knew I had made a mistake in opening that door, but now I would have to come up with something to say. "I'd rather not say," is what I came up with. An explanation that includes mental illness and fears of impotence is one you don't want to give—how could you have more private secrets? "I'm just glad this happened."

She lay back on the pillow and stretched her arms over her head. The bed was big enough that when she did that she didn't touch the headboard.

"What happened to you during all those years?" she asked. "Did you get married?"

I moved a bit to see how sore I was. I was sore as hell. "Yes," I replied. "But I'm divorced."

"Any children?"

"One." This was a subject I didn't want to get into. There were so many subjects to avoid. Poke me and I'd say, *I don't want to talk about that.*

"Did you ever become a reporter?"

"Yes. For a while."

"Why did you quit?" She was on her side again, looking at me, stroking my arm. I wanted to put my hand between her legs.

"I didn't exactly quit. I got starved out. I was getting awfully tired of it, though. You learn after a while that it mostly involves doing stories about pumpkins that look like Abe Lincoln, or asking family members how they feel now that their house has burned down. You spend most of your time feeling like either an idiot or a ghoul."

"Umm. Sounds like your kind of business all right."

I touched her breast. My hand stayed there, stuck, like a metal filing to a magnet. "I've got to leave," I said, despite the way my hand felt about it.

"Why?"

"I've got some things to do. And I can't take being this close so soon."

She stared at the ceiling and looked disgusted about something. I assumed the something was me. I always assume that.

"You've got to take it easy," she said after a moment of silence. "The doctor said he didn't think you'd been seriously injured, but you're supposed to remain in bed for a couple of days and you're supposed to see a doctor if you feel anything unusual, like sharp pains, or if you see any blood in your urine. He says you really should go to the emergency room."

"Gee, I don't think the company wastes its money on insurance," I said. "I'll take it easy." I kissed her forehead and started crawling out of the big bed. "Boy, I thought you had a nice neighborhood. You know, I think you ought to look into some kind of security service."

"I'm going to. I've never had any trouble before."

I continued to work my way out of bed. I had always liked king-size beds, but it felt like it took me five minutes to get to the edge. I gently lowered my feet to the floor. I didn't feel like dancing.

When I had dressed, she said, "I'll see you." She was beginning to catch on to me. Deirdre was always a fast learner.

"I'll be in touch," I said, no pun intended, and walked gingerly out the door.

My Pinto was in the same place, but it was grouchy from being left alone so long and it crabbed a little before it sputtered to life. You'd think a Pinto would have no pride, but this one did. I did a U-turn and headed down the hill. The radio announcer interrupted the Bee Gees' *Saturday Night Fever* with an overproduced news bulletin complete with teletype sounds and the staccato beeping of a 1948-style news flash. During the past twenty-four hours the absent-minded bandit had struck twice and once had nearly been caught because he became engrossed in an article in the *National Enquirer* and was reading it while the grocery clerk collected the money. The clerk had to remind the robber that this was a stickup. The clerk complained to the police that the bandit also stole his personal copy of the *National Enquirer*. The radio announcers were having fun with this story, and between chuckles they were implying that the police had better have a lead on this master criminal pretty soon.

I waited quietly at the cab stand outside the Oasis Rooms, shifting carefully now and then to ease the pain in one part of my body or another. It was early evening. I had had two fares and nothing had happened at Gandalf's. I wondered why I was doing this. I could leave Wendell Mercer in hiding forever if I wanted to and could then enjoy the company and charms of his wife. A relationship with Deirdre was a pleasant possibility, though I had reservations about it. What she saw in me I couldn't see, but so long as she saw it I could take advantage of it. Having a wealthy and attractive woman interested in me couldn't hurt my self-image. Why I wanted Mercer back under these circumstances was beyond me. Perhaps it was to settle things, put him aside once and for all. Perhaps it was because of my natural tenacity. I was a detective now, even though I probably shouldn't be, and this was my job. But my new career was upsetting a carefully ordered life, a life which included little naps at the cab stand. So, as was usual whenever I started to think things through, I became bored, turned the two-way radio to full volume, stretched out my legs and dozed.

I woke to screeching and yelling over the radio.

"Forty-one!" the dispatcher shrieked. "Are you asleep out there? I finally get you a fare and you don't even come on the air."

"Forty-one," I said blearily. I hurt like hell and didn't give a damn what the dispatcher thought. He gave me an address and I quickly wrote it down on my log. I glanced over at Gandalf's. It was closed. Oh well, I would make a little money for a change.

The call was a special—a request for my cab number—at a restaurant on the south side of the Spokane River. The river runs through the center of the city, is wild and beautiful in spots. It's one reason the city exists at all, because it provided power to the early industries. There's still a little hydroelectric dam right in the middle of town, and its spillway is a tourist attraction. The restaurant, near the dam, was "post-hospital." It had not existed before I was sent to confinement in the rubber room, but was suddenly *there* when I returned to town. It was in an area of Spokane that used to be interestingly run-down until the city fathers spruced it up for the 1974 World's Fair a few years ago. The restaurant was classy, a place I would have avoided for its oak table, candlelight, and fern ambiance. The people who frequented the place tended to wear Calvin Klein and Pierre Cardin.

I stopped in front and a young, dark, curly-headed sophisticate staggered to the cab and climbed into the rear seat. He was good-looking and obviously a young man of taste, someone who had just walked out of *GQ*. I disliked him immediately, and wondered why he had chosen my number. It was 1978, so he was probably a numerologist.

"Where to, Bub?" I asked.

"Bub? Bub? I haven't heard that since my uncle the potato farmer died," said the man, settling into his seat, looking drunkenly insolent as he stuck a cigarette into his mouth, let it droop, and lit it with drunken panache.

"Sorry about your uncle," I said. "Where would you like to go, sir?"

He mumbled an address located in a better area of Browne's Addition, then tossed the spent match to the floor—not bothering to extinguish it first. I was glad he was still back there with it, because at least he cared enough to stomp on it after it began burning the carpet. A cab is a dangerous place to drop a match since passengers tend to leave a lot of flammable trash behind.

When we were on our way, he said, "Know what I'm going to do tomorrow?"

"Prostate operation?" I ventured.

"You're quite a wise-ass, aren't you"—he looked at the license on the visor—"Moody."

"I try."

"Well, you can't spoil my mood. I'm joining one of the best law firms in town tomorrow."

"I'm delighted for you, sir," I said, though my British accent definitely isn't the best.

"You're pretty hot shit for a cab driver. I mean, what would a guy like you, probably with some college and brains, be doing driving cab?"

"You've got me confused with someone else," I told him. "I'm not the guy with the college degree, though I have a license to kill—a cab license."

"Seriously," he said, "I mean, you look to be thirty, thirty-five. Don't you want any money, respect, women?"

"I don't need all that. I have drugs."

"Do you go to school, or have another job besides driving?" He leaned over the front seat so I could smell his Benedictine breath and his Canoë cologne. "I mean, is this all you do for a living?"

"Except for the occasional assignment for the Royal Navy."

"No—really. Don't you do something else for a living?"

"We're home, sir," I said, hitting the brake a little hard so that my friend lurched forward at about warp seven, but managed to catch himself before being hurled into the windshield.

"Three-seventy-five," I said.

He thrust a crumpled five at me. "I hate guys like you," he said, almost spitting. "Guys who could do better but go around like they're better than you because they're poor. I'm not at all like you, Moody. I'm not stupid. I'm going to have it all."

And with that he left and invaded his homeland, a pillared mansion of an apartment house where I supposed he was known as Snookie.

As for me, I figured I had done enough PR for the company for one day.

For a few days I mostly settled back into my routine. I didn't hear from Sheila or Deirdre or Nat, and I kept to myself. I didn't even take Sunday off as usual, but just kept working, partly because I needed the money and partly because I figured I'd better keep the vigil at Gandalf's. Just to make myself feel like I was pursuing more than one lead, I began to look into Mercer's property assets. I thought he might have found some little hidden piece of rental property—a small house or an apartment—where he was hiding out. I spent a couple of hours each morning at the tax assessor's office. This was located in a county building that looks like the castle at Disneyland. A nice little old lady helped me search through the records for property under the various names Sheila had given me. We found only a few, and none of them looked promising as hideouts, but I copied the records and organized them into a folder for possible future reference.

My nights were spent at Gandalf's with equally bleak results. It began to look like I might have to tackle 1313 Olympus again or call in the police, until one Tuesday evening.

I was sitting at the cab stand reading *The High Window*, only half paying attention to what went on inside Gandalf's. I'd had my fill of bookstore intellectuals when I was a student. I glanced up whenever someone went in or came out, and that was all. I was healing from my wounds of the other night, but I was still sore and out of sorts. I wondered from time to time about my assailant, but I didn't think about it too hard. It just gave me another good reason to stay away from Deirdre's house.

At about nine o'clock a man walked up the sidewalk on Gandalf's side and turned in at the store. He was five-ten or so, wearing a peacoat and jeans with cowboy boots, and he was carrying a briefcase. It was the briefcase that caught my attention because it was an expensive one—leather with brass trimming. I looked again after he was inside the store in the commercial fluorescent light. He resembled Wendell, but I couldn't be sure since I had only seen a couple of mediocre photographs. I called in to the dispatcher and signed out of the car for a bathroom break. Truth was, I wouldn't have used the bathroom in the Oasis if my bladder had been the size of the Hindenburg.

I walked carefully across the street, still feeling pain in my kidneys from where the guy had hit me the other night. I entered Gandalf's and moseyed over to the Grove Press shelf to browse through books that would have depressed William Burroughs. I leafed through *Last Exit to Brooklyn*. Occasionally I glanced over my shoulder at the man in the peacoat, who was studying the comics and poster art. He stared a long time at each picture. I looked back at my book.

Good old Hubert Selby, Jr. This kind of reading had been a lot more interesting for me back when I was a student, back when I had had the philosophical equivalent of a frontal lobotomy performed on me by the English and Humanities Department. It was something they tried to do to every student so there would be less criticism of the kind of bullshit they peddle.

I noticed that a girl standing nearby was looking at me covertly from time to time. I had made a mistake. I was looking at the same type of thing she was interested in, and she was giving me a signal that I could say something offhand like, "Isn't Camus fantastic?" or "Don't you love Ionesco?" and then we could go to her place. These intellectual types are very depraved. They prefer a guy who can discuss *The Flies* intelligently, and yet looks like he just got back from a five-year hitch with the Hell's Angels. With my nose I qualified on the last point. But my "Born To Lose" tattoo had worn off. I gave her a phony smile and walked over to a rack of Harlequin Romances, an anomaly at Gandalf's but a fortunate one as I would be safe unless some secretaries arrived.

The man in the peacoat studied the comic books ever so carefully, checking the dates, artists, and writers. I could see him clearly from my new position and was almost sure it was Wendell Mercer. He had the thick glasses, the stupid look, and the dark hair, though it was longer now than in the pictures. If it was him—and I wasn't positive—I didn't want a scene in the store. I wanted to do this quietly for Deirdre's sake. With another glance at *Shadow of Love*, I returned it to the rack and walked out. I signed into the cab, did a quick U-turn, and parked it across the street in front of the store. I was illegal as far as the cab company was concerned, but at the moment I didn't care. It would give me a chance to keep my eye on Wendell—or his clone.

I didn't get a fare, and he didn't leave until they closed at ten. The girl who had been looking at me came out first and this time didn't give me a glance. Cab drivers don't turn them on. Then a long string of intellectuals and weirdos trailed out of the store, clutching pearls of wisdom written by psychopaths, paranoids, and manic-depressives. After that the clerk locked up.

Wendell was in the middle of the others and I planned to follow him down the street to a likely spot, then confront him. If he was soft, as he had appeared to be in the photos, I figured I'd have no trouble getting him to go with me. But instead of continuing down the avenue, Wendell walked up to the cab and climbed in on the rear passenger side, pretty as you please. It was like having Judge Crater walk into your office and tell you he could find Ambrose Bierce.

When he got in, I noticed what was different about Mercer. He had shaved off his mustache.

It took him a minute to settle in and then he said, "I'd like to do a little shopping. Take me to the quick-mart at 21st and Ash."

That was an interesting request, and I decided to find out what he was up to. I wasn't going to let him out of my sight, and before long he would be delivered home.

On our way up the hill, my passenger said, "Are you cool?"

This was underground lingo for "Can I smoke a joint in your cab?"

"Sure," I answered. "In high school I was voted most likely to be cool."

Wendell lit up. It was Colombian or something as strong.

"Toke?" he asked.

"No, thanks. I gave it up for Lent."

"No shit? Did you really?" Guys who are stoned

are like that. They wouldn't know sarcasm if it bit them in the ass. I just drove without answering. Wendell had obviously made some changes since the last time he was home. Spending three months with Julia had affected him. Heiress Patty Hearst had been kidnapped by the Symbionese Liberation Army and had returned home as a machine-gun-toting revolutionary. After his absence this realtor would return as a pot-smoking, comic-book-reading hippie.

We got to the store and he said, "Pull up on the side here," pointing to a spot that was out of sight of the front of the building. He was digging something out of his briefcase.

"Wait here," he told me. "I'll be right back." And he tried to get out of the car. It was the car I'd had the other night, the one with doors that didn't open from the inside. I opened the door for him, and he moved stealthily, if unsurely, toward the front of the store. He was holding something in his pocket. If this turned out to be what I thought, I'd have some tales to tell when I became a grandfather.

I waited a minute or two, then I climbed out of the car, walked to the edge of the building, and looked into the front window. Sure enough, there was Wendell at the counter holding a .45 automatic on the clerk. The clerk looked pretty rattled and he was digging through the drawers of the cash register getting the money out. At this hour Wendell didn't have any chance at the safe. One other person was in the store, a little old lady digging through the freezer compartment. She didn't seem to notice that a robbery was going on, but I had a feeling that if she had noticed she would have been in favor of it. Seventy-three cents for a package of peas, indeed.

So Wendell was the bandit. I wondered if Julia knew about this. Perhaps she and those other goons were involved.

I understood now why the bandit was absent-minded. When you screw yourself up on Colombian before a stickup, it must make things pretty interesting, both for you and your victims. Even as I watched I could see that his mind was straying and he was reading the back of a box of Lucky Charms as the clerk dug up the money. The man finally had the cash collected and I could see him try to get Wendell's attention to remind him that he was in the middle of a holdup. Wendell finally noticed the clerk's efforts, jumped backward as he recognized the situation, and waved the gun around a bit. He looked about ready to exit the store, so I returned to the cab.

Wendell came out of the store like a gazelle on Quaaludes. He looked behind him, right and left, then climbed into the cab. I heard him stuff some things into his briefcase and close it. "Thirteen-thirteen Olympus," he told me, "and make it quick." I pulled out of the lot and sped east. I figured it would be the way least likely to be clogged with cops. Wendell sat quietly in the back, still half in a stupor. He didn't notice my route or that I wasn't exactly heading for the north end of town. I got down into the commercial district near my home and turned up a dead-end alley.

"What are you stopping here for?" he asked. Without answering I reached over the seat and grabbed the briefcase from him. I was opening it when I heard him say, "I didn't put it in there. I put it in my pocket," and I felt the barrel of a gun against the side of my head. The briefcase lay open in my lap. A paper sack of money rested on top of a bunch of underground comics.

"What are you going to do?" I asked, half afraid and half bothered by a smell in the air.

"I'm going to split," said Wendell.

I recognized that smell now. It was cheap plastic, like they make toys out of. And toy guns. I glanced to my right to make sure. The gun was definitely a toy. It wasn't even the right color for a real gun. I could see where the barrel had been molded together.

"I kind of doubt it," I told him, and reached back for the toy pistol. He didn't struggle much. He slumped back in the seat, defeated and resigned.

"Who are you? You gonna turn me over to the fuzz?"

Fuzz. There was a word I hadn't heard in a long time. This guy was stuck in the 1960s.

"I'm going to do a lot worse than that, Wendell."

"How do you know me?" He leaned toward the front seat and studied my face. "Jeez, what a nose."

"Yeah. A lot of people like it."

"Noses are really incredible, aren't they?" he said, waxing philosophical. "They're really amazing. Did you know that noses don't have any bone in them? Only cartilage?"

"They have a little bone," I said, caressing my veteran proboscis. "And although I find talking about noses fascinating, Wendell, what I want to talk to you about is your disappearance and your career in crime."

"What a bummer. Man, you going to take me to the cops?"

"No, Wendell," I said a little testily, "I'm not going to take you to the cops. I'm going to stay with you until you're straight, then I'm going to drop you off with your wife."

"Hey, man, who *are* you?" He studied me again through his thick glasses, then, not learning anything, he looked at the floor and mumbled, "Hey, man, that's not fair. You can have all the money. Just let me go. Oh, man."

"Not only am I not letting you go, Wendell, I'm going to charge you the full fare for this trip. It's going to come out mighty close to your take in that little grocery store back there." I picked up the microphone and called in. "I've got a guy who just wants me to drive around awhile."

"Lucky you," said the dispatcher.

"All right, Wendell. We're going for a little ride. You up to it?"

"Oh, man."

I pulled out of the alley, and started cruising north on Division Street. While I was driving I counted the money. Eighty-seven dollars. Not bad for one fare. I figured on traveling till we had used it up.

After a while Wendell seemed to come down a bit, though he was still way up there. I said to him, "It would help if you could explain how you got into this situation."

"Well, who are you, man? Jesus, I'm glad I'm not on acid."

"I'm a private detective hired by your wife to find you."

"Oh, man."

"You say 'Oh man' one more time and I'm going to throw up."

"Oh, man."

"So why didn't you turn up at work three months ago? Or was it four? And how did you end up at thirteen-thirteen Olympus?"

I could see Wendell in the rearview mirror, wetting his lips. Maybe he was on more than just grass.

"I was really tired of all of it, you know. I just wanted some space to be myself. I was tired of work and Deirdre. I just felt trapped, man. I met Julia. She was wonderful. She told me over and over that I ought to try acid, that I would see things differently on acid, that it would expand my consciousness." Wendell was looking out the window as he talked, like a sightseer on a bus tour. "I didn't try it until that last morning, that morning when I was walking to work a few months ago. I ran into Julia. We went for coffee. We talked about work and that I really didn't want to go. I wanted to spend the day with her. Man, she's a great lady.

"So she pulls this package out of her purse and says she has something sweet for me, and inside there's this cube of sugar.

"I didn't take it right away, but she kept after me and pretty soon I did. She's so different from Deirdre. I trusted her. She's a good lady, not like Deirdre. I just never had any control with Deirdre. She told me what to do, everything."

Wendell lapsed into silence for a long time and finally I said, "So you were walking to work and ran into Julia and . . ."

"Man, can I have a joint?" he asked.

"No. Just tell me the story. I'll give you a cigarette."

"I don't want a cigarette."

"Sorry, it's all I've got."

I lit a cigarette. I used to smoke only at home. Now I was beginning to carry them and that was a bad sign. I had turned off Division heading west and we were up north on the bluffs overlooking the river. It was a beautiful night. As a detective I was in seventh heaven. As a man I was a little lower than that, maybe fifth heaven.

Wendell had apparently given up his demand for marijuana and continued. "So I took this sugar cube she gave me. I thought it might be interesting and maybe I'd go to work high. I'd already tried grass with Julia a couple of times and it was fun." Wendell paused for effect, as if the next thing he had to say would blow me away. "It was *windowpane acid*, man. I was so high I could hardly walk. Julia had to lead me away from the restaurant. She took me out to her house. She put me in this room with a mattress and black-light posters and a strobe light. Then she turned on *Pink Floyd*. We stayed there for about twenty-four hours. I kept looking at the ceiling because there was this calendar up there. Julia said it wasn't really there, but I saw it anyway. I checked it against the little calendar I carry in my wallet and it was perfect, a regular calendar— except it was in my head and I was projecting it onto the ceiling. It had the years too. I could see my whole life running out and all I was doing was selling houses and going to cocktail parties and doing what Deirdre told me to do.

"But the weirdest thing was that I was visited by ghosts, like in that Scrooge story. I felt their presence. I knew they were around."

"The ghost of Christmas past?"

"Hey, I'm not kidding. They were real people, people I knew, people I had heard about, people I thought were dead—like my dad. And the others too—the ones . . ."

"Which ones?"

"Never mind. Just people. They were in the room with us. Julia tried to tell me I was just having hallucinations, but I *knew* they were real—I *knew* they were visiting me—trying to get back at me. It scared me. I knew I had to change my life.

"I knew I couldn't go back to my house. It just freaked me out too much. I mean, the thought of Deirdre scared me. Deirdre would want me to keep on doing what we were doing. Oh, man, you're going to take me back there, aren't you?"

"Just relax. It won't be so bad when you're straight," I told him. I was a little alarmed at the intensity of his objections. "She just wants to get divorced from you, that's all. She just wants it settled."

"Deirdre divorced?" Wendell started a little spasmodic laughing jag and between bursts of laughter he said, "You don't know Deirdre at all. Who are you, man?" He kept laughing until it wore off and he settled into distraught silence again. I just kept driving, trying to pretend all this wasn't bothering me at all. The night was nice. The road was good. There was no traffic. What the hell did I care what happened to Wendell Mercer? What did I care if he had ghosts too?

"There's Bud and that crazy guy, too," he mumbled after a bit. "What am I going to do about them?"

"What? What are you talking about?" Crazy guy? That sounded like me.

"Nothing man, just leave me alone. Just give me my money and let me go." He said it forcefully and he moved toward the front.

"Easy, Wendell." I hit the brakes and he slammed into the seat. Then I hit the gas and threw him the other way. He sat back, dazed, trying to get his bearings. He was still high on something and it was a good thing for me. I began to think about taking him home. I didn't want him to suddenly go out of

control. After he had settled down a bit I told him,
"I don't want any trouble, Wendell, but I'm prepared to handle it. Just go on and tell me the rest
of the story. I'll see that you're treated right. I hope
you can get this straightened out and go back to
Julia or whatever you want to do—except rob grocery stores, that is. How did you get started on that,
anyway?"

"Bread," he said tonelessly.

"You have all kinds of money," I protested.

"Not in hiding. I didn't have *any*. Besides, it was
a statement as well. I never hurt anyone, never
even used a real gun. We sat around nights talking
about all the people ripping other people off—you
know, the lawyers and doctors and realtors.

"And the people they're mostly ripping off are the
poor. I thought about those little grocery stores.
They're just taking all that money from the poor
with their high prices. Did you know that most of
their customers are black and poor? I just thought
I'd liberate some of that money."

"Did you ever think about cab drivers?"

"Huh?"

"Many of their customers are poor and black.
You never thought about robbing cabbies, huh?"

Wendell thought about it. "You know, man,
that's true. I never thought about it before." Then
he dismissed it with a wave of his hand. "Naw, they
don't carry enough money. Besides, they're just the
tools of more powerful people."

"Did Julia or any of the others know about this?"

"No. I was going to tell them eventually. Not right
away. I didn't know how Julia would take it. They
didn't know."

"Wendell, my meter's running up. I think I'm going to take you home." I crushed my cigarette in the

ashtray amid all the bubble gum left by the former driver.

"Do you know what a hassle that's going to be?"

"You want me to take you to the police instead?"

"If I go back I've got a lot to atone for, a lot to make up for. I've got to correct some things." Wendell sat with his head down, his hands folded on his lap. He studied a spot on his peacoat.

"What are you collecting all those comic books for?" I asked as I wheeled around and started for the South Hill.

"Because I like 'em," he said, sounding like a kid whose TV privileges had been removed.

"Is that the kind of art you're into?"

"I do some of that. I saw that stuff the second time I was on acid. This is the kind of thing I missed back in the 1960s because I was already out of college and working when it all started. Julia and I went to a bookstore downtown—Gandalf's. Do you know it?"

"That's where I picked you up."

"Oh. Anyway, it was the first time I read a book in a long time. We bought one and went to a coffee house and I read it from cover to cover. It took about four hours. I collected books, but I never read them. I haven't read a book since college."

"Did you break into your house the other night? Your old house."

"Yes. I picked up a few things. What I really wanted was to take my Mercedes. God, I miss my Mercedes. I wonder if Deirdre would let me drive it."

"That's how we figured you were still around, you know."

"From my Mercedes?"

"No, dummy, from you breaking in the other night."

"It was a mistake. I really wanted those things, but it was a big mistake."

"Well, you can have it all back now."

"Yeah, sure, man. You don't know, man."

"It'll work out," I said, sounding like a social worker. "It'll work itself out and you can go back to Julia."

"Maybe. I can just tell them I'll keep my mouth shut and go along and everything will be okay."

"Yeah." Whatever the hell he meant by that. We were near his street now. I turned onto a small road a block or so from the house, and we neared the climax we were both waiting for. We pulled up in front of his former mansion. He looked like a pauper about to meet with the Lord High Sheriff.

I got out and opened both passenger-side doors, retrieving the briefcase but leaving the money and his toy gun behind.

"C'mon, Wendell. Now, remember, I'm going to hang on to this money. All you have to do is take off without leaving a proper address and I'll send the cops after you—you'll end up in jail for five years for those little jobs you did. All I ask is that you stick around until this is settled. After that, I don't care what you do." He climbed out of the cab and stood with his hands crossed in front of him like he had handcuffs on. He was coming down off whatever he was on and he didn't like it much. I led him by the arm to the darkened house. It was nearly midnight.

I rang the doorbell a few times, then we stood on the porch in the darkness for a minute or so, me looking at him and him looking at his feet. The cab waited by the curb, its engine running and its lights on.

The porch light came on first and Deirdre opened the little window in the door. "Oh, it's you, Scott," she said and opened the door. Then she froze with her mouth open and stared at her runaway husband. She was wearing an elegant robe and still looked good though it seemed we had pulled her out of bed.

"Wendell," she said finally, surveying him up and down with disgust, perhaps at the clothes he was wearing. She looked at me, a mixture of anger and victory on her face. "Come inside."

We followed her in, poor Wendell all contrite and limp as a fish. There were some tears on his face and a kind of frightened look about him. I felt sorry for the poor bastard.

We walked in a line into the huge, sumptuous cavern of a living room.

"Sit down over here," Deirdre told Wendell. I hung back as he sat where she directed—on the sofa. Wendell was a man surrendering to his fate. He was emotionally exhausted from being stoned, from the relief and despair of being returned home. He waited, looking at his feet, for Deirdre to begin. She sat on the arm of the sofa and leaned down. Then, as if speaking to a child she said, "*Why* did you *leave* me?"

He didn't answer.

"You left me with all the financial problems," she said. "You left me with Bud."

"You're better with financial problems." He said in a sulking tone. Then, giggling quietly, he said, "You're better with Bud, too."

"Very funny. Now you're back, you're going to have to deal with Bud. You've got to straighten things out now," she told him.

"Things will never be straightened out," he said. "And I don't care about money anymore."

"Sure, you don't care about money because

you've found religion or something. You don't care about money because you've always had money. Some of us weren't so lucky."

"I'm not lucky," Wendell said in a way that made me feel sorry for him. "I don't think I'm lucky."

I walked away from them at that point, wandered to the other side of the room. I could still hear, but I felt less like I was intruding. I listened while I spent my time looking in the drawer of an occasional table, hoping to find a cigarette to smoke. I still didn't carry a full pack with me and always ran out just at the moment of greatest need.

"Your parents gave you money," Deirdre continued.

"Just enough to start a business," he responded.

"More than I was given."

"Not enough to keep it going when we got into trouble."

Deirdre fell silent.

I had found a package of Salems in the drawer and took one. I looked at Deirdre and Wendell once more as they sat together silently. I had heard enough of the conversation. I didn't want to know more about the man whose wife I had slept with. I slipped out of the room to the den and phoned Nat's home. A woman answered.

"Is Nat in?" I asked.

"He's asleep," she told me.

"Wake him," I said. "He'll want to talk to me."

A few minutes later I heard his voice. "Shoot," he said.

"This is Moody. I brought Mercer in tonight."

"You found him?"

"Yup. I located him downtown. We're at his house now."

"Well, it looks like I got me a number one private

eye," Nat said. "We can get this thing settled now. How are you going to be sure he stays around?"

"I'll be here tonight if it's okay with Mrs. Mercer. We'll keep an eye on him until you're ready to handle things."

"Right, okay. Just try and convince him it's not going to help if he runs out again. All she wants is for him to give her a decent settlement, then they can separate. He can live wherever he damn well pleases then. I'll be up in the morning to see if I can get the paperwork rolling. Tell him he'll need a lawyer."

I hung up and returned to the living room. As I entered, Deirdre was asking in loud voice, "*Who? Who did you live with?*"

Wendell wasn't answering. He was a teenager who had been asked to rat on his friends and he was refusing. Deirdre turned to me. "Who was he with? Where did he live?"

"I don't really know," I told her. "I picked him up downtown."

She looked at me with that look that said she didn't believe me, but wasn't going to pursue it. Wendell looked up at me with an expression of gratitude. He seemed to be pleading to be taken out of Deirdre's presence.

I suggested Wendell might be better off in bed for the moment. That got her steamed up again. "Why should he have any rest? I haven't had a good night's sleep since he left." Then she blushed and looked away. "Yes. Okay. I want you to stay though, and make sure he doesn't leave again."

"He won't leave. Will you, Wendell?"

He shook his head. "No, I won't leave," he said.

"Excuse me a moment," I said to Deirdre. "Give me a yell if he makes a move." I left the room and walked to the bathroom. I searched through the medicine cabinet and, sure enough, Deirdre had sleeping pills. I doubled the dose called for and brought them into the living room cupped in my hand.

"You were always weak," Deirdre was telling Wendell. "You never could face up to your decisions. Once they're made you have to live with them, that's all."

"I feel like having a drink," I interrupted. "How about you two?"

Deirdre nodded. Wendell shrugged.

I walked over to the bar and poured three scotches. I emptied the capsules into his drink. I stirred it with my finger—I didn't think Wendell would mind.

I handed out the drinks, making sure Wendell got the right one, then we all drank. Wendell looked like a drowning man.

A few minutes after we had finished them I motioned Deirdre over and asked, "Do you have a bedroom upstairs—one he'd have trouble getting out of if I was watching him?"

"Yes."

"Good. I'll take him there and get him settled in. I think he'd stay even if I didn't watch him. I know something about Wendell that should be helpful in keeping him here. We won't be able to hold onto him by force for very long, though. He's got rights."

"What do you know about him?"

"I'll tell you some other time," I said. It might change your image of him, I thought. It took guts to do what he did—even if it also took a little dope.

"Wendell," I said, and he looked up from his empty drink. It was hanging from his two hands. "Come on. You might as well go to bed." He put his drink down and stood, followed us like a puppy, up the stairs and down the hallway.

"I remember this," he said, as we walked. He was with us physically, but his mind still seemed to be orbiting Pluto.

I checked the bedroom and it was two stories above the ground and the large windows didn't open. It seemed safe enough. There was another gigantic bed like the one in the guest room downstairs. I removed anything I thought Wendell could use to kill himself, including a few mirrors and sharp objects.

The ceiling was high and the light fixture didn't look strong enough for anyone to hang from. It was a depressing thought, but that sort of thought was my specialty, so I considered it.

"You need to use the bathroom?" I asked.

He shook his head no.

"You'd better go anyway," I said, knowing how long he'd be out.

He went and I stood outside the open door. Then I followed him to the room and watched him go in. He looked at Deirdre and me like a kid being put to bed and said, "Good night."

"Good night," I said, and he closed the door.

Deirdre and I stood around in the hallway for awhile.

"Are you going to stay out here all night?" she asked, looking confused.

I told her about the sleeping pills.

"I guess it was the only way," she said after a moment. We waited awhile, then I knocked on the door. There was no answer. I opened the door and Wendell was stretched out sideways on the bed, his peacoat half off. We straightened him out and began undressing him.

"You know why I'm so mad at him, don't you?" Deirdre asked. She was pulling off a cowboy boot.

"I didn't think about it much," I said, struggling with a shirt button. "I just got the impression you were a little pissed."

"I was worried about him," she said, almost in tears. "I was mad because he left me with everything and he hurt my feelings, but I was also worried about him. I'm not a complete bitch."

"I never thought you were," I lied.

"I knew he wasn't happy this past year," she continued, "but I never thought he'd leave me like that, just up and go. I don't understand it."

He probably couldn't get a word in edgewise, I thought.

I said, "There was more involved than just a decision on his part. He was on acid when he left. That can make you a little funny, especially the first time."

"Acid? You mean drugs? LSD?"

"Not hydrochloric."

"I wish you weren't such a wise-ass."

"So do I." We had him down to his underwear now. I lifted him at strategic points as she pulled back the covers. Then she pulled them over him and looked down at her sleeping boy.

"I'd like to stay with him a minute," she told me, staring at him. "Then I want you to tell me where he's been." There was a tone in her voice that indicated she might be a little pissed at me too. I walked out of the room and waited in the hall. I was suddenly tired. I wanted the safety and comfort of my sleazy apartment.

I stayed for another half hour, and then I told her I had to leave. I had been distracted by our drama, but suddenly remembered my cab, still out front, lights on, engine running.

"Leave? I want you to stay. I can't handle him alone."

I thought she could handle a dozen Wendell Mercers, but I said, "He'll be out till at least ten. I'm only going to be gone for a couple of hours. There are things I have to do."

"Why did you bring him in the cab? Is that still out front?"

"I'll explain that later," I told her and walked out the front door. She watched me from the doorway as I drove away.

I signed in with the dispatcher, who had apparently been trying to get in touch with me because he screamed in my ear a little. He screamed a little more when I told him I wanted to come in for the night.

"The bars will be closed soon," he said. "We need drivers out there."

I agreed to stay out for the bar rush, and I did. The cab was in the lot at three a.m. and I turned in my money. Wendell's money was with it. My threat to Wendell had been no more than a bluff. I didn't want anything to do with his career in crime. On the other hand, I didn't want to return his money and in the process get myself jammed up with the police. I took the pistol with me, and when I was out of the lot I tossed it into a field. Some kid would find it and get a heck of a kick out of it.

Then I went by 1313 Olympus. Some lights were still on. I figured they might be. They would be wondering about Wendell. I wrote a note explaining that Wendell was safe and that it would be a good idea if Julia didn't try to contact him for a while. I included my name and phone number. It might be inviting trouble, but I thought she had a right to know what had happened to him. There were so many ambiguities to this business it was hard to decide what to do. I stuck the note on the front door, then headed back to Deirdre's.

The lights were still lit as expected, but I didn't see her in the living room. I found her in the hallway outside Wendell's room. She was going to make damn sure he stuck around. She was agitated.

"I didn't think you were ever going to get back," she said.

"I had errands to run. How's Wendell?"

"Sleeping."

"I want to check him, then I think we can go downstairs. We can watch the stairs from there anyway, though I doubt we need to."

I turned on the lights in the room and looked at Wendell. He was sleeping peacefully, the sleep of the drugged. Beads of perspiration covered his brow. I doubted he was dreaming, but if so he would be having nightmares. Just for the hell of it I checked his pulse. It was fine.

I turned off the lights.

"I'm so tired," she said as we left. She leaned her head left and right, forward and back, exercising tired muscles. She led me to the living room. She left me there for a few minutes while she went to make some coffee. Then we sat on the couch, she at one end, knees curled up beneath her, I at the other, slouched down with my legs stretched out, and we drank the coffee.

She sucked on a cigarette and let the smoke come out her nose. "Do you remember that time you came over to see me when you were riding a bicycle drunk? You were riding around in a circle talking to me, but because you were drunk the circle got smaller until you just fell over."

"Yeah, I remember," I said, though I didn't. You remember less about riding a bicycle drunk than if you were sober. And you remember less of your life generally after once having gone mad.

"I wish I were still a sophomore in college," she said sadly. "I wish we were still kids going to school and we didn't have to worry about any of this. My parents took care of everything and I didn't have to do anything but play. I didn't have to worry about money."

I looked around the luxurious living room. It seemed a funny thing to say, especially since what I remembered of her father was that he was an Irish plumber who seldom had enough work to make ends meet. I always figured it was what made Deirdre more than a little interested in the acquiring of the green. As for me, I was a working class socialist— too proud to pursue wealth, preferring instead to merely hate those who had it.

"I think we ought to go to bed," I said. "It's going to be a long day tomorrow. We want to be up before Wendell."

"Okay."

She looked at me, questioningly.

"No," I replied. "I'm going to stay on the couch, if that's all right."

"It's all right." It was four-thirty in the morning and she still looked beautiful. I probably looked like Quasimodo with a hangover.

She walked out of the room for a moment, then returned carrying a blanket. She handed it to me.

"Good night," she said, leaning down to kiss me on the forehead.

I stretched out on the couch. "Can you get up by eight?" I asked.

"Sure."

"Wake me, okay?"

She nodded and left me with my insomnia. I knew I wouldn't be able to sleep for some time. I have this problem on my day off, too. I can't get to sleep until six a.m. no matter what I do. I tossed awhile, foolishly trying the impossible, then I got up and wandered around until I had located a pack of Salems and lit one. I wanted this day to end, but it wouldn't go away. I wanted this whole affair to end, including the one with Deirdre. She was too good for the Moody of today. Fifteen years ago it was all right, going to football games, getting drunk on wine and beer, playing with one another in the back seat of my car. It had been a simple adolescent relationship—we didn't know ourselves, much less each other. She saw me as an attractive, philosophical English major, and I saw her as an attractive, stylish girl with wit and brains and very soft skin. Since then I had matured into an attractive, psychotic, unsuccessful, brooding man. And she had matured to a . . . what? Upper-middle-class, serious, disappointed . . . what? I wanted her to nurse me back to health, but how could that ever work? I couldn't ask that of anyone, but especially not Deirdre. Her hard edges had become even harder over the years, and the financial success overpowered me. Around her it was difficult to excuse the failure in myself.

I sat for awhile, reading *House Beautiful*, feeling as relaxed and at home as a gerbil on a roller coaster, then curled up on the couch dreaming about Wendell Mercer. In my dream I was holding him hostage. Keeping a man against his will, no matter how rightly, grated on my nerves.

I woke at eight when Deirdre kissed me gently and caressed me. She had a way of sneaking up on me. I returned the kiss but then pulled back and held her away. I felt like I had slept with a restless bulldozer.

"Wendell?" I asked.

"Still sleeping."

She made coffee and we continued our vigil.

Wendell still wasn't up when Nat Goodie arrived. I had a quick conference with him. He was cheerful, dressed in a three-piece wool suit and carrying a leather case. We met in the study where Wendell kept his book collection.

Nat was grinning from ear to ear. His face was smooth and full of guile.

"Nat, I think I want out at this point," I told him, still clutching a cup of coffee Deirdre had just given me. I stood by the tall windows and Nat sat comfortably on the edge of the walnut desk. The desk was equipped with objects from the 1930s—an art-deco lamp, a pen set on a marble stand, and several ornate paperweights. One was a pair of hands clasped in prayer. A prayer for Wendell, I thought.

His grin didn't waver. "You did a good job, Moody. If you want out, that's okay. You promised to try and find the guy, not babysit. I got someone who can come by and watch over him. As soon as we get a lawyer in here for Mercer, this won't take long anyway. All we've got to do is get some papers served and be sure we know where he's living. We're okay now." He rose and clapped a hand on my shoulder. "You did good. Drop off the bill and we'll pay you right away. I'll have plenty of other work. You surprised me."

"Mercer'll be okay?"

"He'll be fine. He's just got to help us clear up this mess and all will be well."

"All right. I'll hang around until your man gets

here."

"Good. Fine. Hey, man, you're beautiful."

"Yeah." But I felt like Mr. Hyde.

I hung around until Wendell was up and Nat's man and another lawyer arrived. Wendell didn't look like himself, at least not the one I'd known. When he came down the stairs he was wearing an expensive suit. He looked like he could close three deals before breakfast. I don't think the clerk at the quick-mart would have recognized him.

Nat had had a conference with him while he was dressing and I wondered if that was what had given him the sober look he wore. He looked at me but didn't nod or show any sign of recognition. He didn't look pissed at me, but he should have.

As time passed more people arrived, most of whom I didn't know, but one was Bud Baum. Everyone took turns having a conference with Wendell in the den. The rest of them stood around in groups in the living room chatting, drinking wine and coffee, and nibbling on cakes and cheese. It reminded me of an art show opening, but the center of attention was being roasted, not toasted. I didn't want to look at his face again unless I had to. It was about eleven when I left. Deirdre saw me to the door.

"I'll give you a call," she said, but I had a feeling things were over now. We both felt the weight of what had happened, and was about to happen. She was going to be preoccupied for a long time and I had caused it all. This kind of success wasn't as much fun as I'd imagined it.

"You going to be all right?" I asked.

"I think so," she said. Already she was more distant. She may as well have been Andromeda.

"See you."

"Goodbye."

I walked down the steps to my Pinto and drove off. I didn't realize how badly Gary Cooper felt in all those westerns when he rode off into the sunset. I wasn't even doing that. I was driving a Pinto into overcast midmorning indifference.

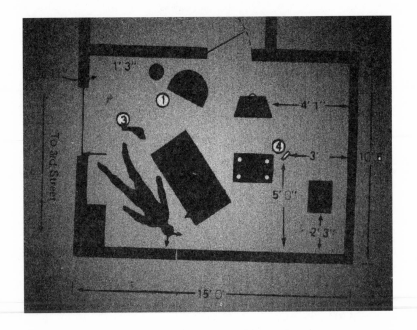

CHAPTER FOUR

I turned in my bill the next day, and a few days later I got my check. I didn't ask how things were going with Wendell. I didn't want to know. On Friday I called the psychologist and made an appointment for Monday. Something was depressing me. When I found out the only appointment was at nine in the morning I was a little more depressed. I woke at eight, had a cigarette, and lay there depressed. When I got out of bed, I wrenched my back. I wasn't having a Sealy Posturepedic morning.

By the time I was in my car heading for Houston's office I was almost late, and then I got behind this guy who was driving his car like it was an egg and he didn't want it to get cracked. Then, every time he stopped at a light he was doing something on the seat or floor of the car, arranging something or writing something. Some people consider driving a part-time assignment while their real work is emptying the ashtray, doing a research report on the seat, or looking around on the floor for a lost Kleenex. He was one of those.

I got to Houston's at just after nine. Alma was apoplectic. "Dr. Houston has been waiting for you," she said as I walked in. I was surrounded by setters, Persians, wire-haired terriers, and dental patients. Alma was being unusually assertive and there was a look of determination on her hawk face. She was both angry and terrified that I would disappoint Dr. Houston. I ignored her, went over to the door to his office, and knocked.

"Who is it?" he asked.

"Scott Moody."

"Oh, Scott. Come in."

I went in and seated myself across from him. He was looking particularly old today. Maybe the entire world was in a funk. "How are you?" he asked, fixing me a cup of sugary coffee.

"I feel like shit," I said.

"What's the problem?"

"Every time I come in here you say, 'What's the problem?' Can't you think of anything else to say?"

"You *are* testy today," he said calmly, handing me the coffee.

"And this coffee's too goddamn sugary," I told him, handing it back.

"Good. That's good, Scott. You've never corrected me on that before." He poured me another cup and sugared it up like the first one. This time I didn't say anything about it.

"So, what's the problem?" he asked.

I rolled my eyes upward in a display of frustration, then looked at him with disgust. He had his jovial Santa Claus smile on his face.

"I'm pissed off."

"That's not too unusual for you, Scott. At least not in *my* observation." He picked up his pipe, stuck it into his mouth. Naturally, he didn't light it.

"*More* than usual," I added.

"What's the problem?"

I was beginning to develop a nervous tic near my right eye. "I took that case I told you about."

"I remember."

"Well, I solved it."

"Congratulations. I'd think you'd be happy."

"I was, but now I don't think I like the way it turned out. The guy I brought back is miserable. I feel guilty as hell."

"Didn't you think about that before?"

"I just thought I wanted to be a detective."

"Even though you got the idea to be a detective during a psychotic fantasy, you must have realized as you got better that all professions in the real world have a mixture of good and bad about them. In my profession I've had people commit suicide after I've treated them. I had to recover from the guilt. You have to see that part of it was his fault. He was the one who ran away. Naturally, they were going to try to find him. You just happened to be the one hired to take care of that."

"I suppose you're right. I still don't feel good about it. I'm wondering if I should get out of this work."

"Maybe. I think it's pretty stressful for a guy with your disposition and past problems."

"I got involved with the woman, too."

"That's good."

"No, that's bad. I probably won't ever see her

again and I feel worse than I did before about women."

"It's a beginning. Growth isn't always fun."

"You should write aphorisms."

Houston smiled. "What would you say to this woman if she were here and you were honest with her?"

"I'd tell her she's a real bitch and I hope I never see her again."

"You have an emotional involvement with her, even if it's negative. Why are you mad at her?"

"Because she made me feel again. I didn't want to feel."

"You didn't think you'd ever feel again, something besides emptiness or anger?"

"Imagine a gorilla sending flowers," I said.

"What?"

"If you can imagine me as a warm, caring, and optimistic human being, you should be able to imagine a gorilla sending flowers."

"They'll come back to you whether you want them or not—your feelings, good and bad. You feel something for this woman, even if it's anger. I suspect the anger is because you cared, and still do."

He may have been right, but what the hell difference did it make to me? I just shrugged, let my eyes drop.

"Forget about the man you brought in. He'll be all right. He's getting what he deserves. It's not your fault. You just did your job. Isn't that right?"

"That's right," I said with emphasis. "The bastard had the effrontery to want out of his life. He just wanted to enjoy himself. The poor bastard."

"I don't think you should be a detective," Houston said. "I wondered about that from the beginning. I think you need to be involved with people in a positive way."

"I thought it would be romantic. You know, hard, cynical private eye cracks cases that defy solution. I thought I was cynical enough for it—I mean, if not me, who? I didn't expect to have any more feelings about it than I do about anything else."

"You know that's a child's view, don't you, Scott?"

"So—it's a child's view." I put my chin on my chest and sulked. Fucking grownups.

"By the way, Scott. While we've got a minute, I've been wondering about something since you started coming here."

No, not that. "What's that?"

"What happened to your nose?"

"I got hit by a baseball."

"Scott."

"Some guys in Times Square beat me up."

"Scott."

"If you already know, why bother to ask?"

"I don't know for sure, but I know it was something that happened in the hospital."

Reluctantly I nodded an affirmation. Right now I hated this guy. He always picked something humiliating as hell to talk about. "I got beat up by another inmate, if you must know."

"Patient."

"Inmate."

"Why?"

"Because he was crazy, that's why. Big guy. He didn't like people who wouldn't follow his orders. Since I never follow orders I was a natural target. The funny thing is, he wouldn't have hurt me if I hadn't been betrayed."

"Betrayed?"

"By the people inside my head. You know, the

people I talked to."

"How could they betray you?"

"That's hard to explain. They let down their guard."

"I don't understand."

"Join the club."

"No, explain it to me."

"When I was crazy I had these *powers,* I really did. Now don't misunderstand. I don't mean I could fly or anything like that—though sometimes I probably thought I could. I just mean I was capable of extraordinary physical things."

"*Supernatural* powers?" Houston looked a bit alarmed.

"I thought so at the time, but not now. It was more that I could do subtle things with my hands and body—I had a kind of precise control over my muscles and over physical objects. You know how people say we use only a fraction of our brain—it was as though I had the use of 100 percent. It sounds kind of stupid, but when I turned the pages of a book I could feel *each* page precisely—never getting two pages stuck. I could draw automatically—just put my pencil on the paper and my hand would create a beautiful picture. I didn't try, but I'm sure I could have juggled a dozen eggs—I had such ability at times—with the help of my internal team."

"How does this relate to the fight at the hospital?"

"Well, one of my abilities was to defend myself. My hands would seem to know what to do without me thinking about it. I noticed it first when I was wrestling with deputies at the jail. They had to get extra men to control me. I was unusually strong during this period, and if someone tried to hit me I could fend off their blows. That's how I prevented myself from getting hurt when I fought with the deputies at the jail."

"You fought with the deputies?"

"Sure. I didn't want to stay in jail."

"Okay. So how'd you get your nose broken?"

"I was in the dayroom—the area where they let crazy people *socialize*—and this guy started telling me to do something. Naturally I—"

"—Talked back."

"Yeah. He didn't like it, so he attacked me. At first I was okay because even though he was bigger than me I was able to block his blows with my forearms and hands. *I* didn't really do it, of course. It was the people inside. They moved my hands—just kept blocking him, no matter what he did—as long as he directed blows at me. I was lucky that he didn't grab me or try to choke me. I probably couldn't have defended myself against that."

"So how'd your nose get broken?"

"I was doing fine at first—I was scared, and I wasn't in control, but it looked like the people inside were going to be able to fend him off until he got tired or gave up. Then, just at the last moment, my arms were jerked down by my side. I didn't do it. It was a very strong involuntary motion—like someone had grabbed me. While my arms were down, he gave me a nice solid punch—right in the nose. It happened just before the orderlies grabbed him, so he wasn't able to do any more damage. I had the feeling that the people inside decided to punish me a little."

"That's an amazing story."

"Crazy, huh?"

"Yes, and no. It makes sense to me. But I'm a psychologist."

"It still makes no sense to me." I noticed I was getting sleepy. When I'm really upset I can't sleep very well. "This must be working, Doc. I'm feeling a little better already," I said.

"You want my honest opinion?"

"If you're going to give me an opinion, that's the one I want."

"I think you have a long way to go."

I slept, but the case was still on my mind. Later that afternoon it was more on my mind because I got a call from Julia Baldwin. When the phone rang I was dreaming about talking doughnuts. Big, mean, cynical doughnuts. I thought they were pretty cute. I wondered if they had a sister. I woke up knowing what I was going to have for breakfast. I picked up the phone, and sat down at the living room table.

"Scott Moody?"

"That's right."

"This is Julia Baldwin. You kidnapped my friend."

"I didn't kidnap him. I just took him back home."

"I don't agree. You screwed him over, mister. I tried to call him and they wouldn't let him talk to me."

"I didn't have anything to do with that. Hey, all I did was locate him and take him home. You'll probably be able to see him in a few days."

"They say he doesn't want to see me—what a crock."

"Who's they?"

"His old lady and some man. I called twice."

That would be Deirdre and perhaps Nat or

Bud—or the other man they left to babysit. I leaned back in the chair. "I don't know what to tell you. It wasn't my intention that he be held prisoner. Perhaps he's just changed his mind. What he was doing wasn't very responsible."

"Responsible? What he was doing was worse—it was criminal."

"What are you talking about?" I wondered if she knew about him robbing the convenience stores. "Look, I know you don't like realtors very much, but—"

"I don't care what you think, creep. I just want you to know I intend to get Wendell back. I want to know if the lawyers or the police or any creep other than you knows where we live."

I thought about that for a moment. It seemed best that someone else know—for health reasons. "Yes," I lied, "I gave that information to Deirdre's lawyer so they could trace Wendell again if they had to."

"Asshole," she said, doing little for my already bruised ego. "Now we'll have to move." She hung up.

I held the dead phone to my ear for a moment, then lowered it to its cradle. I had just come out of my depressed mood and now she had put me back in it. I decided to leave my apartment just in case the troops from 1313 Olympus would be visiting. I had a cigarette, dressed, and went for coffee and a doughnut. Then I went to work early.

When I got back to the apartment the next morning I found it in a shambles. Though it had been specifically demolished it looked only a little worse than usual, except that Irving, my philodendron, had been smashed to the floor and the table had been destroyed. The phone had not been ripped out of the wall though, because it was ringing. As I answered it I thought to myself that someday I would have to clean this place up. I stepped over the dirt and Irving's corpse and picked up the receiver.

"Scott?" a panicky voice said, even before I had the chance to be rude. "Mr. Moody?"

"I'm Moody," I said.

"Scott, this is Deirdre. You've got to help me. Wendell is missing again."

"Missing? Since when?"

"He took a phone call early this morning. Then he left. There's been no one watching him for a day now—he seemed back to his old self so I thought it would be okay. But he got into his car this morning and drove away before I could stop him."

How'd he get the keys from you? I wondered. "Do you have any idea where he might go?"

"None. I thought he might be at the office, but I can't raise him on the office phone. I don't know, maybe he's there and not answering. You could check. But if he's not there he might have gone back into hiding. You're the only one who knew where he was when he was missing. I need you to help me look for him."

"I'm leaving now," I said, and hung up the phone. Apartment cleaning would have to wait. I would check the office, then I could cross the Maple Street Bridge on my way north to 1313 Olympus.

As I was nearing the office I saw a Mercedes parked along the street. It was metallic reddish-brown, the same as Mercer's. When I drove by the office, there was no movement inside and no lights were on. Apparently they didn't open until later. I pulled around the corner and found a parking space. Perhaps Wendell was in the back, practicing the old workhound habits Deirdre wanted him to return to. Keys were hanging out of the lock on the front door. When I pushed, it opened. I stood in the darkened office looking at the rows of desks. I listened for voices or any noise. I heard nothing. I made my way cautiously to the back of the office and began opening doors and peering in.

I opened and closed the door to the third room, then stopped. I had seen something I didn't want to see, something totally out of order. I opened the door again. A shoe protruded from behind the desk.

I got a clammy, chilly feeling on the back of my neck and shock waves from my nerves passed up and down my limbs. I walked behind the desk and saw Mercer. A reddish-black spot was spreading onto the floor from beneath his chest. His arms were splayed at abnormal angles. The acrid smell of body fluids choked the air of the closed room.

I made it into the hallway before I threw up, bent and kneeling from the spasms. I wanted to get as far as I could get from the sight of that gray face and that smell. When I could control my stomach, I sprinted to the toilet. I was in there a long time. Though I finally got over my nausea I couldn't slow down my breathing. I felt my own death was imminent. I wanted a tranquilizer. Before the breakdown I might have handled this a little better.

When I felt relatively under control again I flushed the toilet. I took some paper towels with me to clean up the mess I had made in the hallway. I'm not all that hygienic, but I felt there was enough of a mess without my adding to it.

Then I used a phone in the front office to call the police. I told them what had happened, who I was, and that I would be waiting outside.

When I walked out the door to the sidewalk, I noticed that the sun was shining. I sat on the steps, relieved to be away from the sight of that body. I couldn't really remember what Wendell looked like lying there with no life in his body, with the flaccid muscles of death, not thinking, not moving, not living. I could, instead, see myself like that and it terrified me, not for myself, but for my daughter, who needed me, no matter how worthless I might be. I sat on the steps sobbing.

I was still sobbing when Sheila arrived. Embarrassed, I tried to control my emotions. Her panty hose rustled, her brown dress shone in the sun. Gold glinted around her throat. A leather bag hung loosely from her shoulder. Cars droned by on the busy street. The occasional driver stared at us.

"What's wrong, Scott?" she asked.

I sniffed a bit, took out my handkerchief and wiped my nose. I stuck it back into my jeans and straightened my cord jacket. "It may not be open for a while," I told her. "Your boss is in there and he's not in very good shape."

"Mr. Mercer? Or Bud?" A puzzled look crossed her face. She stood there holding the strap to her shoulder bag, looking like someone waiting for a bus.

"Mercer," I said. "He's dead. In there." I pointed my thumb toward the office. "Someone shot him."

"Oh, my God." She sank to the steps beside me. Her dress rode up her thighs. She fumbled in her purse, came up with a cigarette. I took it from her.

"Do you mind?" I said, and lit it.

"No, I guess not." She found another and lit it with a match.

Bud Baum arrived next, in a tasteful—for him— dark brown leisure suit and white shoes. It looked like a day for fall colors. He seemed annoyed when he saw us sitting on the steps.

"What's going on here?" he asked. His hair ruffled in the light breeze. He looked like an ad in a

Sears mailer—a few years old. "Sheila, you're supposed to open up. And what are you doing here, Moody?"

"Something's wrong, Bud," Sheila said, diffident but firm. "Mr. Mercer's been shot."

Bud looked shocked. "Wendell? But I just spoke to him yesterday. He seemed fine. He was back to normal. Is he . . . ?" His voice trailed off as he pointed toward the office, and Sheila nodded that yes, he was. We had to move over to allow him to sink to the steps and slump there beside us.

We sat there for ten minutes without saying much, Sheila's hip massaging mine, before the police arrived. Then they seemed to be coming from everywhere. I thought they must have gotten together down the street to plan it, the way it worked out. Cars with lights flashing pulled up onto the curb, in the parking lot, down the street. Then an unmarked blue car parked in front and two detectives in suits got out. The driver was an older guy, a paunchy Rod Steiger sort, as he looks lately, lots of wrinkles and flesh and curly gray hair under the hat. The other was short, Spanish or Italian, with a choirboy face and a small mustache. They approached us as an ambulance stopped in front. By this time the street was pretty well blocked off and officers were directing cars to other routes. People had gathered on the sidewalk from nearby offices and stores, and were talking quietly and looking in our direction. The three of us sat there.

The short detective approached. "Which one of you is Moody?" he asked.

"I am."

"You found the body?"

"Yes."

"Show me where it is. Bleaker, find out who

these other people are." The detective spoke with a soft purring voice.

We all stood up. I opened the door. I would show him where it was, where the poor dumb bastard I had brought home was now. I wouldn't like it, but what the hell, I didn't like anything. Garcia followed me to the rear of the office and I pointed through the doorway.

"How did you happen to be here?" he asked, his voice as polite as an undertaker's.

I explained the call from Deirdre, gave him my background in the case.

"Private investigator, eh?" He looked me up and down, his nose flared. I figured that meant he wasn't impressed.

"My name's Garcia, Lieutenant Garcia. I want you to tell me about finding him. Show me where you went, what you did."

I showed him and told him. Another officer had joined us by this time, and he was taking notes. After about half an hour of this, Garcia took me to his car and opened the back door—the one with no handles on the inside. "I want to ask you some more questions. Wait here, I'll be back in a few minutes." I got in and he shut the door. I didn't like it in the car. It reminded me too much of the other time, when the police had taken me into custody for "being a danger to self and others." I consoled myself that I was in my right mind this time—as right as it got anyway.

I watched the scene from my back-seat vantage point, like a dog waiting for his master to return. Evidence teams taped off the area and began working. Mercer employees, a dozen or so had arrived, were separated from each other and questioned one at a time.

Garcia came back after what seemed like an hour and began asking me questions—*What was I doing here? How did I know Mercer? Where was my car? Which car was Mercer's?* and so forth. This went on for an hour. Then a number of us were transported in patrol cars to the Public Safety Building. I'd rather have been going there for a routine license application. I sat in the back of Garcia's car, squeezed between Sheila and Bud, staring at the plastic shield separating us from the officers.

We were ushered through the lobby of the Public Safety Building, a gigantic marble and granite affair that looked like the inside of Tut's tomb. We cooled our heels in the lobby for a while, loitering and gawking at memorabilia of crime—old pistols and shackles and newspaper stories from the past—enclosed in Plexiglas cases for the public's entertainment. I was singled out for special treatment and taken to Bleaker's office, where I sat waiting for Bleaker and Garcia to show up.

The office was standard bureaucrat—imitation-wood-finish desks, orange carpet, and gray filing cabinets. One of the cabinets was overflowing. When I was alone, I opened it and found it was full of porno magazines. Bleaker had his secrets too. I closed the file, sat on the stainless steel and Naugahyde chair, and smoked cigarettes an officer had bought for me at a machine in the lobby. My lungs weren't complaining yet, and the tobacco helped a bad case of nerves.

After a while Bleaker came in, threw his hat on a cabinet, and started looking around in his desk. "I'll be with you in a moment," he told me. "I have to find these statement forms. I want you to write one. Everything you can think of from the time you woke up this morning."

He gave up on the desk and walked over to a file cabinet. "Now where did I put those damn things?" he said and opened the cabinet. An avalanche of porno peered out at him and he struggled to get the drawer closed again. It was like Fibber McGee's closet, only dirtier.

Finally, he located one of the forms and handed it to me. He explained how I was to fill it out, and then went to do some paperwork on his desk and took some phone calls while I outlined what I knew of the events at Mercer's office. I left out nothing, though I hadn't been too thoroughly instructed on how to go about it.

I was nearly through when Garcia peeked through the door and said, "How's it going, Bleaker?"

"I don't know," Bleaker said, cupping the phone on which he had been conversing with a hooker named Dolores. "How you doing, Moody?"

"I'm just about finished."

"Didn't you send for a stenographer?" asked Garcia, looking pissed.

"Was I supposed to?" Bleaker asked. He was anxious to get back to his call.

"Bring him to my office," said Garcia, disgusted with his partner.

Garcia looked at me. "By the way, you don't mind if we look at your car, do you?"

"What if I did mind?"

"There's always a judge who'll give us permission."

"No, I don't mind," I said.

Garcia left.

Bleaker lit a cigarette, looked at me, and shrugged. "Okay, let's go." He got up and led me out of the office and down the hallway. Garcia was on the phone when I got there. Bleaker told me to hang on to the statement I had been writing and to sit and wait for Garcia. Garcia was telling some superior about Mercer's death. When he hung up the phone, he reached over the desk. "Let me look at this 'informal' statement Bleaker took." I handed it over and he scanned it. After a few minutes, he said, "I want you to do another one, but this time I'll have it transcribed." He called someone and in a few minutes a female officer came in with a recorder and a notepad. That way, I suppose, there would be little doubt about what I had said.

Garcia started asking me questions, using the statement I had written for Bleaker as a reference. He went over every point I had made in detail and from every reference point. Some of the questions were not overly polite.

"You own a gun?" he asked once, out of the blue.

"No."

"So they say," he said. "I checked. You don't own one legally, that much I know. You're pretty new to this business, I gather."

"About a month."

"How do you like it so far?"

"As of this morning I'm not too happy."

"You drive cab, too?"

"Yes. It's my main income right now."

"Well, your documents are in order," said Garcia, taking a wad of gum out of his mouth and depositing it in the ashtray. He waved to the female officer to indicate she was not to include what he was about to say. "There's something about you I don't like. You're a kind of correspondence school PI. I don't like that. I prefer people who have a background in law enforcement."

"I just wanted to be a PI," I told him. "I used to be a reporter. The work is similar."

"The work's similar? That include murders?"

"Sure. I've covered murders."

He leaned his chin on one hand, stuck a fresh piece of gum into his mouth with the other. "Okay, let's finish this interview. I'm giving you fair warning. Everything about your background, your address, your work habits, makes me uneasy. I'm going to do a little more checking into your past and into your part in this incident."

"Okay by me." Just don't be too thorough. **Ex-mental-patient found at murder scene.** Geez, that might mean "case closed."

We continued, but he couldn't pick anything apart. The only thing I hadn't told him that I remembered was about Wendell being the absent-minded bandit. And who would suspect that? As we were talking he got a phone call and afterward he told me, "We couldn't find anyone at thirteen-thirteen Olympus—the house is empty." He paused and cocked his head, "However, we swept up nearly half a kilo of marijuana off the floor. Plus there were a few hallucinogens and nonprescription drugs. You and Mercer have been keeping fine company."

Garcia started the questioning again, gently prodding me for new facts and inconsistencies, me doing my best to walk a tightrope. At the end of it he said, "We'll be calling on you, so you can forget traveling. If you come up with any new information I want you to get in touch with me. If you're contacted by any of these people from 1313 Olympus, I want to know about it. I hope you don't do too much sleuthing on your own, but if you do, I want the results. This is a police matter."

I didn't think it would do any good to accuse him of being nosy, so I just said, "Anything you say."

Garcia bit down on his gum and stared at me intently. He nodded. "That's right—anything I say. You can go now. See the officer at the front desk and he'll get a patrol car to get you back to your vehicle. Just tell him you're a witness in the Mercer investigation. So far, that's all you are."

"Thanks." I left the office and made arrangements for my ride.

When I got to my car it was mid-afternoon. There were still a few officers wandering around outside Mercer Manor, Inc., and the meat wagon was still parked near the front door, waiting to haul Mercer away. It looked like they were going to take all day getting him out of there.

My Pinto, to judge by the arrangement of the debris on the floor, had been searched. I sat there a moment to get my head clear, then headed home. I didn't sleep well, just tossed and turned, inhabiting that agonizing space between awareness and nightmare, a familiar terrain.

I woke in darkness. Sweat was pouring off my forehead and oozing from my chest. I'd had a dream, one I'd had too often before. Actually, it was two dreams. In one, I was dead and was found by my daughter, Allison; in the other, I woke up in the morning to find her dead in the crib. Neither was cheering. I didn't even worry that I was late for work, having overslept. I called in sick, then I called my ex-wife.

"Hello, Andrea," I said when she answered the phone.

"Is that you, Scott?" she asked.

"Yes. I was wondering if I could see Allison."

"You know you can see Allison anytime you want to see her."

"How about tonight?"

"Tonight's fine. I was going to leave her with a babysitter. Would you like to take over? I'm going out."

"Sure." Actually I'd rather have avoided Andrea now that she was dating, but I couldn't go another moment without seeing my daughter, without knowing that she was well and healthy and happy. "Can I come over now?"

"Come ahead. I'll tell her that you'll be here. She'll be excited."

I was holding back waves of depression. "I'll be right there."

I shaved and took a bath, then changed into my cleanest clothes. I wanted to get as much distance between those dreams and me as I could. Then I drove over to Andrea's house.

She lived on the east side, on the edge of a racially mixed area where I spent half my time driving cab. The house was a well-worn white duplex with a run-down yard that the neighborhood dog was filling up with poop. Andrea had been there for about a year, since the divorce, and had taken a job as typesetter for a valley newspaper, a skill she'd picked up during the days we were working newspapers together.

I knocked on the door, noticing the flaking white paint drifting off the house onto the walkway.

Andrea opened the door. It was easy to see why I had fallen in love with her. She had more than a beautiful face. It was an interesting face, with lots of arresting expressions and features—the high cheekbones, wide brow and large nose, a strong chin. She was smiling delightedly at me. Since she had left me she had never held any bitterness. She had left the bitterness to me.

"Scott, it's so good to see you." She leaned forward and hugged me. She's tall, five-ten, and she always felt good to hug, unlike short girls you have to bend down to. She has a fine strong body and an easy manner that made you feel all the more affectionate. I hugged her. I wanted to walk in and be at home. But she'd have to want that too. She would also need to know why I wanted to come back. Though she cared about me, "my daughter" and "safety" might not have been the right answers.

She stepped back and looked at me. "How are you? You're looking good."

"I'm fine, Andrea. How is Allison?"

"Healthy as a chipmunk. She's had a cold, but she's getting over it. Come on in. She's in the living room."

I walked into a jungle of plants. Her house was filled with coleus, Swedish ivy, philodendrons, begonias, baby's breath, Boston ferns, and twenty or thirty other plants I couldn't name. Most of them weren't even placed too high for Allison to reach. Allison had already learned that they were to look at, not to touch.

Allison was lying on the living room floor on a tacky yellow rug I would have liked to replace. She was drawing inexplicable pictures on a pad of newsprint. At first she didn't look up, then she saw me and a look of joy and surprise came over her face. She stood there waiting with her mouth and eyes wide open. She gets that way when she's embarrassed or overjoyed. She was wearing blue bib overalls and a red turtleneck sweater. It was a perfect outfit to complement her baby fat and gray eyes and golden silky hair. Her blue sneakers looked exactly like mine.

"Daddy's here," Andrea said, following me into the room. She said it in a manner that was supposed to increase the excitement of the moment, but there was no need for that. Allison was as embarrassed as she was happy. I knelt and she ran to me, throwing her arms around my neck. I stood up, held her while we hugged tightly. Sobs of sadness gripped me. I was already feeling the pain of the time when I would have to leave. She kept her head against my neck for a long time and I had trouble getting her to look at me. She was embarrassed at seeing me after such a long absence, shy, as with a stranger. I hadn't being much of a father to her lately.

She leaned back, still holding me around the neck, and smiled at my face. She hugged me again briefly, then she grabbed my nose with her hand.

"I'm going to get your nose, Daddy," she said, and pulled her hand away, putting her thumb between her fingers. "See, I've got your nose." She showed me.

"Oh, oh," I said. "Give my nose back."

She grinned and said, "No!" Then she relented when I looked sad, and she put it back onto my face.

"Oh, that feels much better," I told her.

She touched my nose again and this time she pinched it between her fingers a couple of times. "Beep, beep," she said.

"She's been doing that lately to wake me up," Andrea said. "I'll be lying in bed in the morning and I'll feel these little fingers on my nose and then she'll go 'Beep, beep.'" Andrea came up beside us. "She looks more like you every day," she said, "except for the nose."

Allison looked at me. "I'm going to school. I'm getting to be a big kid."

"What are you learning in school?"

"I'm learning to count." She demonstrated by counting to eight, but then her numbers got mixed-up.

I laughed. "You'll have to get those numbers straightened out one of these days, though your mother never did."

"Very funny." Andrea walked around the room picking up some of Allison's toys and clothes. "You should have been here the other night," she said. "Allison had a whopper of a nightmare. She woke up in the middle of the night just scared to death. It took me ten minutes to get her quieted down. She said something was after her."

"It was going to get me," said Allison, a serious and intense expression on her face.

"She said it was big and mean and scary. And do you know what it was?" Andrea asked.

I looked at Allison and she looked back with her best storytelling expression. "It was *toast*," she said.

"Toast?" I laughed.

"It was toast and it was going to get me."

More and more like her dad every day.

"Has Allison eaten supper?"

"No. We were just about to fix it."

"Could I take her out to eat? Just to be alone with her."

"Sure."

I was relieved to hear that. When I first got out of the hospital, Andrea was hesitant to leave the two of us alone together. Not that I had ever done anything weird around her, but as a general statement of distrust of a man who has gone crazy.

We left Andrea at home getting ready for her date and went to a nearby restaurant. We were having a fine time except that I had forgotten children do not behave perfectly just because they haven't seen someone in a long time. Allison was being particularly difficult this evening, but we finally got settled down and I ordered her a grilled cheese sandwich and a bowl of soup, which was all she would agree to eat. About the time the food came she had decided to pour her water into an empty coffee cup at the table, just to entertain herself. I told her she shouldn't do that, she should eat. She looked at me crossly and said, "If you don't let me pour water into my cup, I won't eat my soup or my sandwich and I won't drink my milk."

After the shock of her threat wore off, I said, as calmly as possible, "If you don't eat your food you won't get anything more until tomorrow morning. You won't get any cookies, or bananas, or toast, or anything."

She thought about that for a minute, then said with an alarmed voice, "But—if I don't eat—I'll die."

I almost giggled at that one, it upset me so much. In an even voice I told her, "That wouldn't happen for a long, long time, honey. You would eat tomorrow morning. It would just mean that you couldn't eat tonight and you would be very hungry and your tummy would hurt." I continued eating my meal. She thought about what I said and after a few minutes she began eating.

We returned to Andrea's at six-thirty. Andrea was still alone and seemed to be upset. She found some toys for Allison and asked her to play with them in the living room. That way she wouldn't interrupt us. Then Andrea told me "You were on the news tonight."

"Oh?"

"Yes. Why didn't you tell me about it? You were involved in a murder or something?"

"I wasn't involved. I found him."

"You're a private investigator now?"

"Yes. Part-time."

"I don't understand you, Scott. This isn't like you. This isn't you."

"Who is me?"

"What?"

"Nothing."

"I wish you weren't such a wise-ass sometimes."

"So do I."

"I wonder sometimes whether you're good for Allison."

I frowned and started breathing a little deeper. "You wouldn't stop me from seeing her, would you?"

She thought for a moment. A hell of a long moment. "No. I just don't understand you anymore. You're not the same. You seem to be doing some weird things."

"I've always done weird things."

"That's my point. I was hoping you were over that. Let's drop it. Just be careful. It sounds like you're involved in something dangerous. I hope you know what you're doing."

"I do." Like hell.

I stayed the evening with Allison, playing and romping around with her while her mother went out with a hippie carpenter. It bothered me that she was seeing other people, but I tried to repress my jealousy. So what if he looked stupid and self-centered and boring and she was going out with him though she would have little to do with me.

Allison was up until ten-thirty when I finally got her to give me a kiss and get into her pajamas. Then after she was in her crib she wanted a glass of water, a cookie, and a banana. She got the drink of water and part of a banana, then after a little fussing went to sleep. Andrea got home at one o'clock and we said our brief goodbyes.

"Scott," she said as I was going out the door.

"Yeah."

"Come back more often. Allison needs you."

"I will."

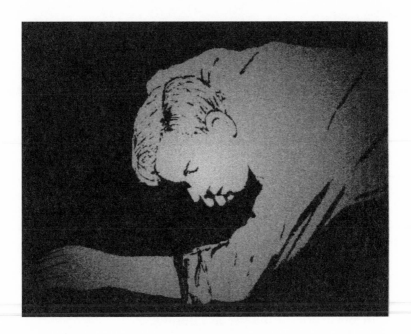

CHAPTER FIVE

When I got home I found a young, blond newspaper reporter camped on my doorstep. I don't mean he was sitting there, I mean he was sleeping crumpled up in a fetal position on my walkway. He had probably been sitting against the tree near my door, waiting for me, hoping to be the first reporter to reach this particular news source about Mercer's murder. Then, at some point during the evening, he had lost the struggle against sleep. He now lay with his notepad clutched between his thighs. A sharpened pencil was still squeezed by sleeping, frozen fingers. A Nikon camera lay in the grass next to him, its strap still around his neck.

I stepped over him, went inside, and went to bed. At about six a.m. he was knocking on my door. When

I looked through the curtains at him I could see he was mad as hell, but at first he didn't notice me because he was reading a sign I had posted on the door. It read: *I don't have anything worth stealing and I don't care if you kill me.*

He looked up and saw me. "What do you mean leaving me out on your steps all night?" he yelled through the window. He had the arrogance and idiot zeal of a recent recruit to journalism.

I closed the curtains and went to fix myself a cup of coffee. I'd nearly finished it before I opened the door and let him in. He was about twenty-five, had brown eyes, a thin face, and a body that looked like it had been thrown together for a weekend trip instead of a lifetime. He was wearing a rumpled tan sports jacket and brown slacks. I greeted him in my old bathrobe—lime green chenille.

He entered, wide-eyed and raging. "You know what? While you left me out there some bastard stole my camera. I woke up and some sonofabitch was staring me right in the face. He said, 'Pardon me,' and ripped the camera right off my neck—not fifteen minutes ago. I chased him, but I couldn't catch him."

"You picked the wrong neighborhood to sleep in," I told him.

"I didn't pick this neighborhood," he said, waving his pencil. "*You* picked this neighborhood. I just wanted to talk to you about the Mercer thing." He ran a hand through his scattered hair. "God, I don't know what I'm going to do about that camera. It belonged to the paper."

"Twenty-five dollars a week," I suggested.

"Oh, no. Never mind that anyway. I want a story. I've earned one."

"Well, I'll give you one then. There was this girl I

knew who had trouble getting dates. I didn't know she was an amputee because when I met her—"

"You're really off-the-wall," he said, looking a little off-the-wall himself. "This is news. This is important. A guy was murdered."

"So what does your rag want to know about it?"

"Who do you think killed him? What's your connection to the case?"

"I thought that had already been covered," I said, then sipped a bit of my lukewarm coffee. I made myself comfortable in my chair while he danced around the room. "I located Mercer. He had been missing for three months. That's my connection."

He inspected the living room and looked into my bedroom. Typical reporter. "Boy, this place is a mess. Looks like someone ransacked it."

"My maid's down with gonorrhea," I told him.

"You want to tell me where Mercer was during his absence?" He had the presence of mind to have his notebook and pencil in hand now.

"That's confidential," I said. "The police know. If you can get it out of them, it's yours."

"They won't even talk to me."

"Taste, I suppose."

"Well, if you're not going to talk, I'll leave. There's more than one way to write a story, you know."

"I thought that was only good for skinning a cat."

"Look, I know you don't want people prying into your affairs. I know you want to keep your privacy. But it looks pretty bad—like you're involved in this whether you want to be or not. I'm not doing this because I want to pry into your secrets. I interview a lot of people, and I don't like hearing their secrets." He was confessing his innermost emotions, a common ploy to get a source to talk. "I just want to understand what happened. It might help you."

"I don't have anything to say," I told him.

He looked ready to give up. He handed me a card with his name and a work phone number on it. "If you change your mind, give me a call," he said. I looked at the card. He was with the *Spokane Voice*, a shopping mall newspaper that came out twice a week. They were trying to convert to a real newspaper by pursuing more substantive stories, perhaps hoping to eventually compete with the *Spokesman-Review* and the *Chronicle*, the local dailies. I stuck the card into the pocket of my robe.

He opened the door and peered out. Something he saw seemed to upset him and he shouted, "Hey, get away from that car. Leave that alone!" He charged out, leaving the door open.

I rose slowly, wandered over, and shut it. Youth. What a horrible experience.

I leaned down and picked up a piece of paper from the floor. It was my check, amazingly undisturbed by the 1313 Olympus gang when they trashed my apartment. For me it was a sizable sum of money. I wondered what I would do with it. Of course part of it would go to Andrea, but there was enough for a little something for me. I was in the mood to buy something, but what?

I thought of Deirdre. I would have to see her today. I just wanted to look into her face after the murder of her husband. I didn't like the immediacy of his death after I brought him back to her. Probably the people from 1313 Olympus had killed him—maybe because of drugs. Who would know?—certainly not me. A nice middle-class boy with the occasional habit of madness would know nothing about the underworld. I didn't know who had attacked me that night at Deirdre's either. Perhaps all this had something to do with Mercer's career in robbery, though whoever had seen Mercer the morning of his death wasn't carrying a toy gun.

But enough of that. What to buy? I thought about it as I pulled on my jeans and a wool shirt, tied up my old sneakers.

By the time I was dressed it was obvious. A suit would be useful. Then I could walk around looking smug and prosperous. I could also get into Deirdre's neighborhood without having someone call the police.

I had breakfast and hung around town until the banks opened, then cashed the check after arguing with the bank teller. She thought I was an impostor because the real Scott Moody had never put that much money into his account. I said, "An impostor coming in from out-of-town to deposit money into another person's account? The weather must be getting to you."

I wrote a check to Andrea and mailed it in the same package with a gift for Allison, a little stuffed elephant. Then I wandered around town looking for a likely place to buy a suit. I ended up at Julian's, a little shop located near one of the fancier and perennially bankrupt hotels. It was the kind of shop where the owner of a Cadillac might go, assuming he had any taste. The salesmen were nice enough to me, though I had the feeling that at any moment they expected they might catch some kind of social disease from contact with someone of my class. The only problem was that I couldn't afford more expensive material than corduroy. I found a three-piece that fit well, then bought a shirt and tie to match. After that I walked down to Florsheim's and picked up a pair of shoes. Nat Goodie would have had a fit if he'd seen me. I felt like Cary Grant out for a stroll, except that I really should have shaved, and Cary had a cleft chin, not a cleft nose.

After I was dressed-up, I felt that I should do something. The something I came up with probably wasn't very smart. I went to see Bud Baum. I wanted to talk to him before I talked to Deirdre. In my present attire I felt I was just about a match for him. I wanted to know if he'd seen Mercer before his death—if he knew any reason someone would want to kill the man. I was still feeling a lot of guilt over Wendell's demise and I felt Bud had answers. Perhaps my new attire would impress him, and he would be more polite and cooperative.

When I walked into the real estate office the first person I encountered was Sheila Woo. She was happy to see me and said, "Ooh, you look nice. You should shave though."

I asked if I could see Bud. She didn't seem too crazy about that idea, but she went to tell him and a moment later I was ushered into his office.

"Good luck," said Sheila as I walked in.

Bud didn't bother with the amenity of shaking my hand this time. He was still sitting at his desk, looking at me with disdain as I sat in one of the chairs across from him. I smiled back.

"Hi," I said.

"What do you want?"

"A little info," I said. "I'm trying to see if I can figure out a possible reason, some motive, for Mercer's murder."

"You have no goddamn reason to be going around questioning anyone," he yelled. "The police are handling this. I haven't any more idea than anyone else, but what I do know I'll tell to the proper authorities, not you."

I was actually shocked by his vehemence, though I shouldn't have been. "I'm feeling a little guilty," I said, quite seriously. "I brought Mercer back just so someone could kill him. I'm a little pissed and I feel a little responsible. I'd like to find out who it was—I'll damn well try anyway. I'm not Catholic, but I have some sense of the word atonement."

"You don't even have a client. You're a creep. And you're getting into police business. I want you the hell out of my office and I want you to leave everyone alone. That includes Deirdre. You hear me?"

"I sure as hell hear you. Probably everybody this side of the river hears you. I'll stay out of your office, but Deirdre is an old friend of mine and I'm going to help her if she wants me to."

"Just a favor to an old friend, eh?" said Baum. "I'll tell you one thing, my friend. You'd better stay away from her. I don't intend that some punk come in here and screw that up for me. Stay away from her, or you'll be sorry."

"I'm already sorry," I said. I got up and walked out the door. "Thanks, Bud, it's always a pleasure."

Sheila looked at me with concern as I walked past. Everyone in the office had heard and was staring. I looked back at them and shrugged. "He broke it off, but now he won't give me my ring back." I walked out the door.

I drove my Pinto up the South Hill to Deirdre's place and parked right in front. I adjusted my suit, walked to the door and rang the bell.

Deirdre came out wearing a red turtleneck and jeans. Her eyes were a little red and it looked like she had been hitting the Scotch again. "Yes?" she said, staring through me. She got a puzzled look on her face. "Scott? Scott! It's you. That's a beautiful suit."

I did an embarrassed sort of soft shoe.

"Come in," she said, and the moment I had stepped over the threshold she held me in an embrace and tried to remove my tonsils by suction. I should probably have told her I had them removed when I was five. My parents gave me ice cream and a red fire engine. Ten or twelve seconds later we somehow ended up on the big bed again. Boy, was I easy. After the events of the previous day I had mixed feelings about it.

Afterward, while we were lying there and she was enjoying a postcoital cigarette, I decided that things were going too well, so I would screw them up again. I was angry at her and I was angry at me. I said, "You always do this sort of thing the day after your husband gets killed?"

"That's a shitty thing to say. I'm upset about Wendell and somehow that made me think of you. I guess I'm infatuated with you and I need the company. At least I did before that remark." She got out of bed and put on a robe.

Now we were both angry at me. Why was I getting involved in this at all? What was she to me? When we had made love the first time, at least I had understood some of it, felt cared about. Instead of turning her down flat as I should have, I had allowed myself to get into this position. I took one of her Salems from the nightstand and lit it.

"Why did you buy that suit anyway, Scott?" she asked as she tied the cord to her robe.

"I thought it would be nice for Wendell's funeral," I said.

She said, "Bastard!" and walked out of the room. I got up and started putting on my now wrinkled suit. I couldn't face tying the tie, so I stuck it into my coat pocket.

I found Deirdre in the living room, smoking and

staring into a wine glass. She had the anxious look of a puppy who's been left alone outside a grocery store.

"I'm sorry I was so rude," I said. "But Wendell's death hasn't done much for my mood." I stood in the doorway to the outside hall.

She looked up. Her eyes were full of tears. "It hasn't done much for mine either," she said. "I don't know how to cope with it. I guess that thing with you was a way of trying. I thought it would be nice to be with you. We had something once. But now . . . what did you come here for?"

"To see you," I said. "To see if you had anything to do with Wendell's death. I know it isn't nice, but I had to know. I knew you didn't care much for him, and right after I brought him back he ended up dead."

"I'm the one who called you yesterday, remember? Does that help, or do you still want to look into my eyes?"

"It helps." I suddenly felt like a creep. The way she was reacting wasn't all that unusual, especially since she'd had little attachment to Wendell—and liked me, I suppose. That was one of the things that embarassed me. I wasn't used to being liked.

I walked behind her chair, put a hand on her shoulder.

"Sorry," I said.

She covered my hand with hers. "All of this is so awful," she said. "Could you stay awhile?"

"I have to sleep sometime," I said. "I'm working tonight."

"You can sleep here."

"Okay." I sat on the couch beside her and held her hand. "I saw Bud today, by the way."

"Why?"

"More curiosity. He said something odd. He implied he had an understanding with you, that I wasn't to see you." I laughed. "I've never been good at following orders."

Deirdre took my news a little more seriously. She shook her head, as if saddened and exasperated. "While Wendell was gone Bud and I went out a couple of times. Mostly he was comforting to me. If we have an understanding, the understanding is more on his part than on mine. He really warned you to stay away from me?"

"He's training an attack dog with my name on it."

"You can ignore that. Bud handles the business, not my private life. I'll take care of it."

"I'm glad to hear that."

Deirdre offered me the couch—her lap, in fact—and I settled down like a child with his mother. I woke several times during the afternoon and we talked, but she never once said, "I can't imagine who could have killed Wendell."

I turned up at work in my suit and when I picked up the keys from the dispatcher he looked at me, wide-eyed but sardonic, and said, "Moody, maybe we should cut down on your commission a little."

I took the keys and my log and hit the streets in number forty-one. For the first couple of hours I had a pretty ordinary night except that I had another special at Spooners, the restaurant where I had picked up my least favorite soon-to-be-shyster. Sure enough, there he was again, Mr. Irregular. He was well-oiled again. He climbed into the back seat, said, "How ya doing tonight, Moody?" and lit a cigarette.

I didn't mind a little unpleasant company if he was paying the tab, but I was curious so I said, "How the hell did you happen to pick my number?"

"It's my lucky number," he said.

Maybe I would have to ask for a different cab.

He wanted to go to the Beef and Brew out on Division. I headed north.

"You look pretty sharp tonight, Moody," he said as we cruised through the traffic, heading north. "Can you afford that kind of suit on your salary?" As usual he was wearing an expensive sports jacket worth more than the cab, though that didn't necessarily make it a top-of-the-line jacket. I usually carried pocket change worth more than the cab.

"I pick up a few extra dollars here and there, Abe," I told him. "Have you graduated from Shuck U, or did they discover your love note to the dean?"

He chuckled, as if I had made a polite joke. It made me wonder if he was from New York.

"That's all right, Moody. I'm a lawyer now and you're still a cab-driving jerk."

"I thought there was a little matter of the law exam."

"I've taken that. These things are too complicated for your little mind, Moody." We pulled up to the Beef and Brew and he got out, a little unsteady from drinking, flushed and red faced, but cute— you know, the kind of guy upper-class twenty-five-year-old WASPs just love to death—missionary style. He insulted me further by over-tipping me when he paid the tab.

"See you again, Moody," he said as he handed me a ten.

"I hope so," I replied. "You're more fun than babysitting a nauseated dog." He grinned a silly, satisfied grin. I pulled out of the parking lot.

The next call was at a grocery store at North-town, a shopping center a few blocks farther north. I figured I was the beneficiary, or in some cases the victim of relationships developed by the other drivers of car forty-one. I parked outside the store in the no-parking zone and waited for a little old lady or drunken shopper to appear. Instead, after I had been there a minute or two, the rear door of the cab jerked open and someone got in. When I glanced in the mirror I started to jump out of the car. I didn't because someone was blocking the driver's side door. It was the tall guy from 1313 Olympus. His fat sidekick was already in my back seat. It was the guy Julia had called Chicken Man. For once I regretted I didn't carry a gun like some drivers did.

"Where to?" I queried, practicing levity.

"Up yours," said Chicken Man.

"Touché." I reached for the radio microphone.

"Keep your hands off that or I'll wring your neck," Chicken Man said.

I kept my hands off it. I guessed the dispatcher could stand the suspense of wondering what happened to me. The thing was, could I?

"Move over to the passenger side," Chicken Man told me. "We're going for a ride."

I moved over and the tall man got into the driver's seat. He threw the car into gear and drove through the parking lot. It was a big parking lot, and waiting near an exit were two women—Julia and a black girl.

They got into the back with Chicken Man.

"Where to?" asked Baby James.

"Anywhere quiet," said Julia. "Just drive around." To me she said, "We just want to talk."

"You wanted to talk the other night when you

took an axe to my apartment, I suppose."

"I was a little pissed at the time," said Chicken Man by way of explanation, sensitive about his reputation for destruction, I guess.

We drove to a quiet side street with no lights and little traffic. It was like the old days cruising around in a car waiting for someone to break out the pot or the beer, but nobody did. As we were cruising around in this neighborhood, Julia talked.

"Look, mister," she said, making me feel ninety years old, "we don't want any more trouble, but you've got us all tied up with the police. We had to move because of you. They think we killed Wendell. We not only had nothing to do with it, but we'd like to know who did. You were working with them—Chicken Man thinks you know."

My stomach began doing jackknifes into a little pool of fear. "I don't know anything," I told her, trying to impress her with my earnestness, my sincerity, my faith in Marxist causes—hoping therefore to save myself from a knee in the groin. "I was hired by a lawyer to find Mercer. I'd like to know who shot him, but I don't. When I brought him back it wasn't my idea that he get bumped off."

"You'd better come up with something better," said Chicken Man, a characteristic viciousness in his voice.

"Chicken Man is right," said Julia. "You clear us with the police or we'll be seeing you again."

"I don't know how to clear you with the police," I answered. "I'm having problems with them myself."

"Look," said Julia. "We didn't have anything to do with Wendell's death. We do have underground connections though, we do have drug connections. We don't want to be exposed to a police investigation. We don't want to be picked up and interrogated. You had better get them off our case, buster."

"You know it's pretty hard for me to get them off your case. After all, they're on my case."

"Maybe you can give them some clues that point away from us. I think the person who did this was someone Wendell was doing business with. I liked Wendell, and when I got to know him I found out something was bothering him, something he did to make money. After he took acid a couple of times he talked about it a lot more. A couple of times on acid he said he started hearing voices, voices accusing him of something."

"Accusing him of what?" I remembered my cab ride with Wendell, and my impression that he was haunted by something.

"He wouldn't talk about it much, but he was upset. I don't know what it was, but it had something to do with business. Just look that direction and you can't go wrong."

"You act as though it were as simple as looking up a phone number. Even if I do suspect someone he's done business with, it's not so easy to find a motive, and a lot harder to actually prove."

"I don't care how hard it is, Fauntleroy," said Julia. "You'd better do it. We want the police off our backs."

"I'll do what I can," I said. "That's all I can guarantee. I'll look into it."

"That's not good enough!" Chicken Man slapped the back of my head the way Mrs. Jewell in homeroom used to when she didn't like my quips.

"Chicken Man, you leave this fellow alone," said the black girl, her accent heavily Spanish, but refined.

"This guy got us into a jam and he can get us

out," said Chicken Man. He lit up a joint and sucked on it. That seemed to quiet him down. I had had enough of him. I wanted to talk to Butterfly Man or Hummingbird Man.

"Drive us back to the store," Julia told the driver. "Drop Adella and me off at the truck."

At the parking lot the two women got out by their pickup, which I hadn't noticed earlier. Then Chicken Man and Baby James accompanied me to the grocery store. This was when I didn't trust them—when they were out of Julia's sight.

Chicken Man got out first and came over to my side. I prepared myself for some parting pain. He opened the door and said, "This ought to keep me in mind," and pulled the pockets off my suit. Then he and Baby James left.

I called in to the dispatcher.

"I had a no-show," I told him when he came on the air.

"When—at the turn of the century?" He paused a moment for effect, then said, "Get a fare over at Imperial Lanes. If they don't show, let me know about it before I grow any more gray hair."

I worked the rest of the night without incident—well, without any more than the usual incidents. When I turned in the car and the money, the dispatcher stared at my suit. "You're kind of rough on clothes," he said.

"Cheap suit," I told him. "They just fell off."

It was seven a.m. when I got home. The phone was ringing. All I wanted to do was to double-lock the door and sleep. Instead I answered the phone.

"Scott?"

"Hello, Deirdre."

"I just thought I'd call to say hi. You told me when you'd be home from work."

"I'm glad to hear from you." Especially after a visit from Chicken Man.

"Drop over later?"

"I don't think I'll be able to today. I don't have too much time during the week usually."

"What kind of work are you doing? Are you on another case?"

"Yes. Not to bring up an unpleasant subject, but when is Wendell's funeral?"

There was a long pause. "Tomorrow."

"I want to go. That all right?"

"Sure. Just no more cracks, okay?"

"Okay."

"Good. I'll see you tomorrow, then." She gave me the name of the funeral parlor, then warned me, "It's a Buddhist funeral."

"A what?"

"A Buddhist funeral. I know it's crazy, but when Wendell was meeting with his lawyers he set up a new will and specified a Buddhist funeral. His parents are going to love it—they're Episcopal."

I was going to love it too. We said our goodbyes and I shuffled off to bed.

I woke at about three with my radio crooning, "Good morning, good morning; Life is sweet with Oroweat; Good morning, good muffin, to you." Only in America.

I had my coffee and a cigarette and remembered to call Garcia about the visit from the people at 1313 Olympus. When I finally got through I learned that he was in a staff meeting and couldn't be disturbed. I hung up and started dressing.

I looked at my suit. That would teach me to be a clotheshorse.

I put on my old clothes and went out for breakfast. Afterward, it occurred to me that I had time to look at one or two of the properties I had located at the assessor's office. Now that Mercer was dead they were of more interest. All of my paperwork on the case was thrown together like a collection of vagrants in a cardboard box in the back seat, so it wasn't difficult to locate the records.

I cruised around looking for the nearest address. It was a squat, two-story building on the north side. There were a number of businesses located in it, making it almost a strip mall. The only one that caught my eye was on the ground floor. It was a fairly large business as far as square footage and had a gaily painted sign that read: *Judgment Day Nursery.* I parked my car and went in.

Inside were children—three and four year olds—playing with toys and Bibles. On the wall among finger paintings and Easter cards was a poster that commanded, *Thou Shalt Not Covet Thy Neighbor's Wife.* One of the kids was wearing a tee-shirt with the legend: *Shadrach, Meshach and Abednego.* A dumpy, pleasant old lady with glasses and a bee-hive hairdo came to the door.

"God bless you," she said, smiling. "My name is Fern Glow. Are you planning on putting your little one in our center?"

"Not really," I replied. "I'm just looking for the owner of the building."

"Oh, my goodness," she said, looking up at me with a dippy *I don't know anything* smile. "I have nothing to do with that sort of thing. I just take care of the children. As far as I'm concerned there's only one landlord."

"You don't know anyone who might know, then?"

"I'm afraid not. I shouldn't be so concerned about things like that if I were you. You should be thinking about eternity."

"I'm sorry, but I really don't have that kind of attention span. Thanks for your help." I turned and left. I looked around at the other businesses, talked to a few people. Nobody could help me. I headed back to my car, then wandered around town until it was time to go to work.

I got up early the next day so I could make the eleven a.m. services for Wendell. I thought maybe I would be depressed about it, but as I dressed, the only thing that affected my mood was my clothes. I combined my old sports jacket with the new slacks and my Florsheims, but the look was a little cock-eyed, like I had been outfitted by Western Auto. It was good enough for a Buddhist funeral, I decided.

Groups of people in black were streaming into Sharon's Funeral Parlor, high up on the South Hill. They carried umbrellas to ward off a misting rain from the overcast sky. I went bareheaded.

I walked inside the stucco building, passing through heavy wooden doors over which a sign read: "Portals of Heaven."

Imagine that. Right here in my hometown was one of the entrances to heaven. I wondered where the gateway to hell was. Maybe it was that little pawn shop down on Main, the one with the proprietor who looked like Boris Karloff.

I filed in toward the back and took a seat with the other mourners. Wendell must have known a lot of people, judging from the turnout. Of course, a lot of them could have been spiritual thrillseekers interested in an Episcopalian who's turned Buddhist. Deirdre was in the front row. I could just catch a glimpse of her blond hair draped by a black scarf.

Next to her was a man dressed in a black leisure suit. He had wavy, graying brown hair. It had to be Bud Baum.

A lot of the people from the realty office attended. They had probably been given the day off. Sheila was a few rows ahead of me, sniffling into a lace handkerchief. She looked better than usual to me and I wondered why. I thought about her long legs and her lips. An aberration in my thinking, I concluded. It would pass.

The ceremony was a long one, with lots of incense and chanting. When the mourners filed by, led by a sobbing Deirdre, I followed. I had thought I was over his death, but when I passed Wendell, I choked up and had to breathe hard to keep from sobbing. It wasn't so much for him, though, as it was for myself and the guilt I felt over his death.

I found the cemetery with the help of a map handed out by the funeral director. We stood around in the drizzle as an Episcopalian minister sent Wendell on his final journey. I guess his family had had second thoughts about the eternal efficacy of a Buddhist funeral. I stood near the rear of the group, pondering my own life and what my funeral might look like, hoping it would be a long time for one reason—Allison.

Then I noticed something odd. At the other side of the group were two faces that didn't seem to belong here. One of them was Julia Baldwin. She was red-eyed and tearful, dressed tastefully in subdued colors. Behind her, carrying an umbrella and wearing a pre-war charcoal suit, was Chicken Man. He gave me a significant look of warning when I noticed him, letting me know I was not to say a word about them.

Chicken Man in a suit. Imagine a gorilla wearing

a suit. That's how it was to see Chicken Man in a suit.

I decided not to say anything. After all, I was only in my thirties—I still wanted to live. And who was I going to tell? Confide to the minister that Wendell's possible murderer was in our midst? I could see Chicken Man killing Wendell. I wasn't sure I could see him firing a gun, not because of gentility but because he'd probably prefer to strangle someone. What would be his motive though? Julia?

When the service was over and the crowd began filing away, Sheila dropped into step beside me. "Hello, Scott," she said. "Are you all right? I haven't seen you since the other day at the police station. Did they give you a hard time?"

"No. I'm okay, I guess. They're not happy with me, but they don't think I had anything to do with his death. How about you?" I wasn't really interested in her answer, but her breasts, peeking out of the top of her blouse, were plenty interesting. The strange thing was, I kept thinking about how I could get her back to her apartment. That didn't seem characteristic of me at all. I had scrupulously avoided women for months. My fear of impotence had made them a depressing subject. Then there was Deirdre. And now my wall seemed to be coming down entirely. Houston would be pleased, but I was appalled.

"They just had us make a statement, then they sent us home." She reached into her purse and took out a package of tic tacs. "Want one?" she asked.

"No, thanks." In my present mood I thought it might help if I had the breath of an elephant.

"It's so sad about Mr. Mercer," she continued, looking down and ahead, but not at me. "He was only thirty-six, you know. He was really a very nice man. He worked a lot, but he was pretty cheerful and good to be around, except for the times when he got depressed."

"Did he get depressed often?"

"Well, every few months or so he seemed to go through a period of really being down. Then he would have Bud run the company while he just moped around. I don't know what caused it, but he just seemed upset somehow, you know?"

The only thing I knew at that moment was that I wanted to smear the inside of her thighs with Crisco.

"He did work awfully hard. You know, he started the business back in the 1960s on almost nothing."

"I thought his family was wealthy."

"Oh, they were, but after they loaned him the money initially, you know, the capital, he built it up from there on his own. He and Mrs. Mercer paid all the money back by 1970 and it's all in their name now—and Bud's too."

"Bud owns part of the business?"

"Oh. I guess I shouldn't have said that. It's just that I feel so comfortable talking to you. I mean, that's not something you should tell anyone, because it's confidential, but it's true. He started working for Mr. Mercer right at the beginning and I guess he bought in after a while. But he's a silent partner."

"Then how did you find out?"

Sheila blushed and I knew she wasn't going to answer that one. An eavesdropper, I suspected. We were at her car and she had a convenient out.

"I hope you'll drop by sometime," she told me as she opened the door. It was a blue Volkswagen convertible. "I'd like to offer you some dinner. Or maybe just a snack. Actually, you could come over right now if you wanted. I'm kind of depressed after this funeral."

Yes, a snack would be nice. "Perhaps another time," I told her, restraining my newly discovered desires. "I have to work tonight."

"Another time, then," she agreed, getting into her car. She rolled the window down, reached out, and squeezed my hand. "Another time." She started it up and drove off.

I stood there awhile thinking about her and about Dr. Houston. I wasn't due to see him for another week, but I wanted to see him now. Something was going wrong. I was in a good mood, cheerful, and excited about life. I wanted to look up Sheila's dress. In fact, I wanted to crawl up it. It was disconcerting as hell.

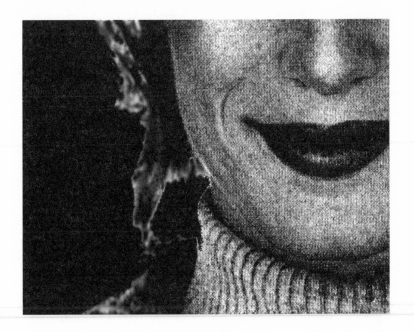

CHAPTER SIX

Houston's eyebrows rose and lowered. He chewed on his pipe and, once, tried to light the end of it like a cigarette. He was more agitated than at any time since I had begun seeing him. I was sipping my usual sugary coffee, but this time I liked it.

"I don't quite understand what the trouble is here," he repeated for the third time. "You've gone to see your daughter and she's fine. You've gone to bed with a woman twice and enjoyed it. It's built your sexual confidence to where you're interested in another woman sexually for the first time in months. It's perfectly natural—good—to feel good. I don't understand what the trouble is."

"I'm just so up," I said cheerfully. "It seems so frivolous under the circumstances. Look, there's a cop downtown who would love to find out about my seamy past, connect me to a murder, and put me in jail. There are a bunch of crazies out there who want to beat me up. A man was killed because I brought him back from hiding, and I'm thinking about being unfaithful to his widow. That's not the kind of situation one should be in and feel terribly, deliriously happy about. I'm afraid something is happening to my brain—again."

Houston puzzled over this for a moment, pulled a few times on his unlit pipe. "Well, it seems healthy to me. The best news I've heard in months. I just wish you would let it happen to you and not worry so much about it."

"I'm not comfortable feeling good. I know a lot more about handling depression than about feeling good. Lately, I've wanted to forget this case and go see Deirdre and Sheila and anyone else I can talk into sex. I don't care about anything except getting laid. I even thought about going up to the South Hill to look around for some phone numbers I threw out of my car."

Houston cleared his throat, ran a hand through his thinning hair. "Well," he said, "now things are becoming a little more clear. This is something I've dealt with before. Your indulging in sex is sport. Your thing is all better now and you want to get back to using it. When you had your doubts about your performance, you thought a relationship with a woman would have to include love. After all you weren't even sure you could perform. Now that you think you can perform you want back into the action." Houston put the pipe down.

"There are a couple of things to be aware of here. You might find that you still have some problems sexually. You've got a lot of mental dysfunctioning, so that's possible. Also, I wouldn't necessarily turn down a relationship with this woman, Deirdre, is it?"

"Yes."

"She could be very helpful to you. What you really need, Scott, to bring you out of this, is love, not sex."

But I was only half listening. I was thinking about Sheila. I was thinking about her ass.

It was late in the morning when I got back to my apartment. As it was Friday, usually a busy night in my business, I planned to spend the rest of the day sleeping. My plans were altered by the unmarked police sedan lurking out front. Garcia and Bleaker waited patiently in the front seat. They both got out when I drove up. Bleaker smiled at me. Garcia chewed gum. They stood in the cold April overcast with their hands in their overcoats.

"Hiya, Moody," said Bleaker, all palsy-walsy. "We been waitin' around for you." He lit a cigarette in cupped hands. Then he put his hands inside his pockets again. He let the cigarette droop from his mouth.

"You have some more questions?" I tried to be polite as a lambchop, but my insides were jumping. Something about Garcia made me nervous.

"We're just a little curious," Garcia said mildly. "We recently found out that you had a prior relationship with Mrs. Mercer."

"In college. That was a long time ago. I haven't seen her since."

"Kind of a big coincidence—you turning up as a novice private eye, then Mercer turning up as a corpse."

Garcia paused, letting me think this over. Bleaker didn't want me to think about it, I guess, because he started talking.

"What we think, buddy," he said with a grin and a tap on my shoulder, "is that you knew the lady 'on the side.' Know what I mean?"

"I know what you mean. It just isn't the truth. I haven't seen her for years. It really was a coincidence. Even if I had a reason to harm him, and I didn't, I wouldn't intentionally hurt anybody."

"You're sure about that?" Garcia said casually as he picked at his ear.

"Yes, I am." I hoped they wouldn't suddenly arrest me. It had happened once in my life—it was no longer something I couldn't imagine.

"Well, if you say so we'll have to take your word for it—for now. But you know, Moody, there's something wrong about you. You seem to me to be a man who's guilty of something. Know what I mean?"

I knew what he meant, but I didn't reply.

"We'll talk again," said Garcia, moving toward the car. Bleaker got in on the driver's side. Garcia climbed in and the car slid away.

I went inside, feeling clammy on the back of my neck and my forehead. I sat in my chair. I stayed there, motionless, for an hour, looking out the window. Then I went to bed.

I got very little sleep before I got a call from Nat's office—his office, not Nat. He was having his secretary call me now instead of doing it himself. She had a few papers for me to serve. At least Nat was still throwing some business my way. Not enough, but some. If I was to continue this PI stuff I would have to have more clients. The business so far had been very irregular. One check was not enough to base a career on. Perhaps if I went to see Nat about it sometime, he would recommend me to some other firms.

I slept, got up, went through my morning ritual, picked up the papers from Nat's office, and drove to work. On the way I heard a news story about the Mercer killing. It was a followup based on a copyrighted story in the *Spokane Voice* written by Ralph Waldo. That name rang a bell, but no one answered. The story gave all sorts of distorted details of Mercer's life in hiding. It told of a gang that had kidnapped the rich realtor, given him LSD and other drugs, then forced him to have sex with one of the ring leaders, a woman named Julia. The writer made the gang sound similar to the Symbionese Liberation Army, with maybe a shade less ideology and brutality. One comparison was clear and familiar—he said the conversion of Wendell from realtor to rebellious hippie was similar to the conversion of Patty Hearst to revolutionary during her time with the SLA. The story also gave some details of his return to straight life and his subsequent murder. The implication was that the old gang had done him in, then gone underground again.

I wondered where they had gotten that story and what kind of trouble it would cause me. Perhaps the police had provided it, since some of the details could have come from my statement—after which they were distorted or misunderstood. When I was talking to Garcia I had made the unfortunate comparison with the SLA. Whoever had been the source had done me no favors. I guess they figured it might be good public relations—there was a lot of interest in the case and pressure to solve it. I thought about Chicken Man. I could see him cracking his knuckles in anticipation of having his hands around my scrawny neck. This case was like a boomerang; the more I threw it away, the more it came back.

The night was a good one for cabbing. I kept expecting to get a call from my underground buddies, but nothing came of that. The sleaze rolled in and the sleaze rolled out. By the end of the night I had had my share of conventioneers, little old ladies, families in town for reunions and the usual drunks, all crawling in and out of my cab from the rain-slickened streets of the city. I thought about Deirdre Mercer's lips from time to time, and Sheila Woo's ass, but for the most part my mood had stabilized to a point about halfway between that of a nihilist and Dr. Joyce Brothers. I turned my money in at six a.m., got to my car, and checked out the papers I was to serve. I steeled myself for a bad morning and planned to reward myself with a steak and eggs breakfast. Judging from my earlier experiences, the steak would probably go on my eye.

I may have wanted a steak, but on my first call what I received was garbage. A fat guy at a ranch house in the valley was taking a Hefty bag of the stuff out to his trash can when I came along and served the paper. He took it, read it, then began swinging the Hefty bag at me. It wasn't strong enough to be used in an assault, so when I came out of there I had the better part of a fruit-and-vegetable salad sticking to the back of my coat. The second guy wasn't that much of a problem as he wasn't home. The third eviction notice was near my place. I planned to make that call, then hit a nearby restaurant for breakfast before calling it a night. I wasn't being paid enough for this kind of work.

The building was a ramshackle brick building several stories high with a broad wooden porch turned gray from age and neglect. It looked like it might have been built around the turn of the century and had a good history before it had fallen on hard times. My party was one Walter Egan in 301. I realized as I entered that this was the same building in which I had called on my old friend James Leach, a very tall black guy who owned a gun. This time they had given me a hard row to hoe if the new client was also a tough guy. I would have to run all the way down three flights of stairs after giving the eviction notice.

I tiptoed down the musty hallway, climbed the creaking wooden stairs, and approached 301. I paused for a moment, then knocked on the faded green door. A rat in a corner of the hallway mistook me for an exterminator, squealed, and scampered away.

The door opened slowly on a heavyset black man whose back was turned away from me. "You kids settle down," he said, and I heard peals of laughter behind him. A frumpy black woman in a pink flannel bathrobe, her hair in rollers, peered at me from the other side of a room in disarray. Thrift shop items were scattered around like the contents of a suburban garage. An old black-and-white TV with aluminum foil for an antenna slumped in one corner.

The man turned to me with a little surprise on his face. He was graying, had a huge nose, and puffy cheeks. There was a large wart on the side of his nose. He wore work pants with suspenders over an armless tee-shirt. Gray hair sprouted from his chest. A musty smell crept from the room, a mixture of greasy food, diapers, and soured laundry.

"Yes, sir," the man said politely and with some dignity. "Can I help you?"

I felt like a creep, but I handed him the paper

and read him my line.

He looked at the document for some time. "Mister, they can't do this to us," he said after he had read it. He eyed me mournfully, studied my face. Perhaps he was looking at the nose. "We're a little late with the rent, but they didn't say they would boot us out into the street. I just ain't working right now." There was a plea for help, but at the same time there was dignity. The man wasn't going to beg me. I didn't know what to do. I had planned to leave immediately, but there seemed no threat and his problem was something I found difficult to walk away from.

"I don't know what to do about it," I told the man, who was staring at the paper again. "I'm just supposed to serve it. I don't want to see anyone thrown out into the street." A little boy peeked around the edge of the door, gave me a terrified look, and disappeared.

"Can't you do nothin'?" he asked. "I hate to ask you, but couldn't you do something? Tell 'em you couldn't find me. I'll get some money somewhere. We can't afford another place."

I took a couple of deep breaths, then wished I hadn't when I swallowed the local odors. "Look," I said, taking the paper back from him. "I'll say I didn't serve it, that I couldn't find you, or you weren't home or something. I'm afraid in the long run it won't do any good, because they'll try to serve it again. It's just a little breathing space. But you can't let anyone know I did this." I wished I was actually doing him a favor.

"Thank you," he said. "I appreciate that."

"That's all right," I replied. I walked down the hallway with one look back. The man was shutting the door and locking it. I felt like Scrooge at midnight on Christmas Eve. Except my ghosts were always on duty.

I got back to the car and sat there a moment. Something about this visit was bothering me and it wasn't just the paper I didn't serve. I looked at the building, thought a minute, then reached back for my box of well-organized records. I pawed through the box for a few minutes before I located the folders with the information collected at the tax assessor. I studied the documents and learned the connection to the building. It was one of Mercer's properties. What a coincidence. I tossed the box into the back and headed to Sambo's for breakfast.

I got to Deirdre's just after noon and saw Bud Baum's Cadillac Eldorado pulling away. His car was lime green. One day someone would have to talk to that man about his taste. If you're going to own anything lime green it ought to be a bathrobe— like the one I have at home. I watched his car glide down the street before I got out of the Pinto. I had no date with Deirdre, no appointment. I just wanted to see her. I had been thinking a lot about her during the past twelve hours.

She came to the door in an elegant royal-blue robe, her hair upswept and pinned. She looked like a Vogue model who'd just come in on the bus from Idaho Falls—travel-worn but beautiful.

"Scott, I didn't expect to see you so soon." She glanced down the street in the direction Bud had gone. "Come on in. Want some coffee?"

"Sure." That wasn't all I wanted, but it would do for a start.

She disappeared into the kitchen and I loitered

in the immense living room thinking it would have been a good location for a scale model of the universe.

"It's nice to see you," she said when she returned with two cups of coffee and a pack of Salems. She put the coffee down on the table in front of the couch and I sat beside her. She folded her legs beneath her, inside the robe, so that she looked like a priestess in a religion whose Bible was a Nieman-Marcus catalog. I sipped my coffee and studied the smooth contours of her face as she smiled impishly at me.

I didn't know what to say to her, didn't know how to have a real relationship with anyone now, but I wanted a physical relationship. I wanted to touch her and be touched. I had had a little practice at that lately and wanted more. She seemed to know that.

After sitting there for a few minutes without saying much I leaned toward her and touched her shoulder. Through the robe I could feel no straps, no restraints—only softness. She leaned in my direction and we kissed. I took some leadership in what followed. For the third time in the past year—and all within the past month—I was soon sweaty and sexually satisfied in the company of a naked woman.

After a few minutes of repose, Deirdre rose abruptly.

"Oh, my God, the curtains!" she said. She moved and I had to move, slid headfirst off the couch as she went to draw the curtains on the front windows and lock the door.

"The mailman had a big grin on his face," she told me when she returned. She was kidding, and we both laughed.

She sat down beside me and we kissed. She was naked and that made me feel like repeating the act. Her body was wonderful for a thirty-five-year-old, though I had little to compare it with. The breakdown seemed to have burned away most of my carnal memory too. She lit a cigarette and put on her robe. Too bad. I dressed and we sat there, all wet, as though nothing had happened.

"That was nice," she said, and exhaled as she returned the lighter to the coffee table. I felt like having a cigarette, but for the moment I wasn't desperate enough to make it a Salem.

I leaned back on the couch, both arms stretched out and my legs extended in front. She nestled against my shoulder and smoked her cigarette.

"Scott?" she said after a moment.

"Yeah?"

"How would you like a job with Mercer Manor?"

"What? You mean be a real estate salesman? Work for you?"

"Sort of. I think the job would be more of an executive position though. Of course, you'd have to train, but then you could move up quickly."

"Work for you?" I asked again, as though I were deaf.

"My company. Of course you'd really be working for Bud."

That'd be great. If I was going to do that I'd just as soon go down to a street corner and put a sign on myself that said, "Kick me in the butt, five cents."

"Why do you want me to work for you?"

"I think you're a classy, good-looking guy. What you're doing now is beneath you."

"You mean being a private detective?"

"That too, but especially the cab driving."

"Oh. You found out about that."

"I dragged it out of Nathan Goodie."

So that was his first name.

"You never did like the idea of associating with people who don't have money—not even when you didn't have money."

She didn't move away, but her voice had an edge now. "Let's not have that argument. We had it enough a long time ago. I think you could do a little better for yourself. And I would feel more comfortable. Thank God there's not a scandal sheet in this town that would make something of our relationship."

"You mean 'Society Dame Dallies with Hack Driver,' that sort of thing?"

"As usual your humor is right off target," she said. "It was just an offer. I won't stop seeing you. I just wish you'd pay more attention to these sorts of things."

My old socialist proclivities were surfacing, but I choked them back and said, "I'll consider it. Give me some time to think about it."

She seemed surprised, as she should have. "You will? It really wouldn't be bad, Scott. You'd pretty much be able to handle things the way you wanted. You'd be a friend of management, after all."

Just like Wendell was. Oh, well. So much for sex and politics. Out of the blue I said, "Do you own a building down on West Third—three hundred block?"

She didn't react much. "We own a lot of buildings. I don't know whether we own one there. Why?"

"Just curiosity. Someone said you own it."

"Who said?"

"Just a guy I was talking to on the street. I don't know how it came up." I reached over for a Salem and lit up. She perched where my shoulder had been, like I was still there. I returned to my place and she leaned on me again. It felt good, but there was tension in the air. For me at least.

"Scott, what happened to your nose?"

It was the last question I expected. "I got it in a fight," I said, too close to the truth. "I was working for a newspaper and we were doing a story on country western music. I was in a bar doing interviews and this guy didn't like 'the tall fag with a notebook.' I got in a couple of jabs with my pencil, but I came out like this."

She was smiling. "That sounds as much like bullshit as your last story." Some women just love men who lie.

"Hey, no, it's the truth. It's that simple. It was a few years ago, over in Montana. I worked on a little paper over there."

"You were married when you lived there?"

"Yup."

"I never thought you'd get married. She must have been something."

"Still is—she has shape and mass. That she is something is inescapable."

"You have a child—girl or boy?"

"A little girl." This was getting too close. I realized now why I had trouble with relationships. I didn't want to share myself—not my real self. Especially not with someone I had any doubts about.

She sighed. "I wish I'd married like that. Simply. I wish we'd had children. Hell, I wish we'd divorced. Anything but to have had it end like this."

There was a sense of sorrow which I had noticed when I first arrived, but now it was more profound.

"Do you know Wendell was trying to become an artist?" she continued.

"I heard. I didn't take it too seriously. He didn't seem the type. But then I don't suppose I saw him at his best."

"He had some pictures in his coat, the one he was wearing the night you brought him home." Deirdre excused herself, went to the den and returned after a moment with the pictures.

"Here's what he was working on," she said, handing me the pieces of eight-and-a-half by eleven bond. "They're awful, but it's touching that he did them. He never showed one sign of interest in art that I knew of."

I studied the drawings—pen-and-ink fantasies colored with felt-tip pens and watercolor. They looked like something by Peter Max through Franz Kafka. It seemed Wendell did have some talent. That much showed.

"What was he like?" I asked. "When he was back home I mean."

"A little quieter than I was used to," she said. "Otherwise, pretty normal. He said he regretted what had happened and he wanted to return things to the way they were. He didn't talk much about the people he knew or what happened to him while he was gone. He wouldn't talk about his art either, although he bought some supplies. They're in his study. He seemed quite changed. In some ways for the better. I never really trusted him though. He was never alone until the day before . . ." She sat down beside me again as I looked at the artwork. "The day before the . . ." She just wasn't going to be able to finish that sentence.

I suddenly wanted out of Wendell Mercer's house. Houston had been right. My up-time had been short-lived. This guy was haunting me and there seemed no way out of it.

"I've got to work," I told her, "I'd better get some sleep before I go on shift. I think to do that I'd better go home."

"Okay." She seemed willing to be alone with her thoughts. We kissed. "I'll see you later. Let me know about the job. Think about it, will you?"

"Sure."

"Chicken Man is pretty mad at you," the voice over the phone said. It was a woman's voice. Other than that I wasn't sure who it was. I was bleary-eyed and foggy after a day's sleep on Thorazine. Why the hell did I always get threatening phone calls while I was still waking up?

"Oh yeah?" I said. That could cover about any situation.

"Do you know who this is?"

"I'm beginning to. Julia Baldwin, right?"

"Are you awake now? I want to talk to you, turkey."

"Shoot." Whoops.

"This isn't very funny," Julia said as I slumped into my only chair, trying to remember what universe I was living in. "We asked you to help clear us."

"Some asking."

"That's just Chicken Man's way. It doesn't matter now. You've got us looking like the fucking SLA or something. We're not. We're vegetarians."

That woke me up. Non-sequiturs are always invigorating. "Hey, I'm not responsible. That story was written by some flaky reporter who got half his facts wrong and he didn't get them from me. I think he got part of it from the police. It might have been from my statement, but I couldn't help that. I made that statement before I was threatened by you peace-loving vegetarians."

"Don't make fun of us, creep. We're not the SLA, but we can fix your ass—Chicken Man can. We still want something from you."

"I hope it isn't my recipe for moussaka because I promised Mom I'd keep it a secret." She couldn't know that my mother died before she had been able to pass on any recipes.

"What a wise-ass," she said. "Look, someone had better clear us. If they start treating us like the SLA, sending out SWAT teams and that shit, we won't have anything to lose. You might though. You and your family."

I looked at a list of the properties that Mercer owned. "I think I know why Mercer was killed—something to do with his financial life. I'll look into it, and I'll try to steer the police away from you if that's possible. But, lady, you stay the hell away from anybody I love. You wouldn't believe how unreasonable I could become if you threatened them. You should know that I've been hospitalized for mental illness. I hope you understand that I can be dangerous."

"We don't want to hurt your family," she said, a little softer in tone. "We just want our lives to return to normal."

You'll need to put someone else in charge of them for that, I thought. "I'll do what I can. Just don't send Chicken Man after me."

"I can't control Chicken Man," she told me. "He's the only one among us who isn't a vegetarian." She hung up, leaving me to ponder the effects of carnivorous behavior. I dressed and went out for steak and eggs.

It was a Sunday, so I figured I could spend the day tracking down Mercer's properties. I wandered around the city for hours, feeling like a realtor searching for listings—except there was no commission in this, just maybe a longer lease on life.

One of the addresses, or what used to be that address, was now a parking lot near the river front. As I recalled it had been there a long time, since an old fleabag hotel had been torn down sometime in the 1960s. Another address was a condominium which had been around for a few years, and another was a restaurant built in the 1970s. It was a fancy restaurant named 'Enry's and I had never been prosperous enough to enjoy a meal there. They specialized in English dishes like blood puddings and mutton and meat pies.

I went inside to see if I could speak to the owner. I found him, a balding man, fortyish with black hair greased and combed to cover his pate. He was in his office paying accounts. I told him I was inquiring about the availability of the property on behalf of another party. He informed me that, while he did not own the property, he had five years left on the lease and there was no chance of a sale. There was not much more I could think to ask as I already knew his landlord, so I left.

It was after I left 'Enry's that I noticed a parade following me. I was getting an escort all over town. Several cars and a truck spread out behind me, passing one another for the privilege of following immediately behind me and one apparently not wise to the other. I figured I was just paranoid at first, but the longer they hung on in the light traffic of a Sunday, the more curiosity I developed. It occurred to me there was a way to check this out.

I headed toward the South Hill, my compadres

following all the way, fighting for position. I got near a park on the South Hill where there's a Y in the road. Unless you really know the town, it looks like a normal dividing point between two equally important roadways. The right-hand turn, however, leads to a parking lot at the park. I turned in and circled around. The other three vehicles came into the parking lot in succession and we all circled for a moment. When they realized what was going on, all the people in the vehicles began looking embarrassed, covering their eyes or looking away. It must really hurt your pride when you're tailing someone and get into a situation like that. Behind me were what looked like two cops in an unmarked green sedan. They were young and dressed in sports jackets. They looked like the cops you saw on *Police Story* or *CHIPS*. They were the coolest of the bunch. They parked and walked over to pretend to look at the ducks. If they'd been really good they would have had something to feed them besides bullets.

Behind them Chicken Man looked very paranoid and searched for an exit. He kept glancing in the direction of the cops. The last car was one I had never seen before and the man inside was a stranger as well. The car was a red BMW. The driver was wearing a cap and glasses so I couldn't see him well, but took him to be an out-of-towner lost in our big city. Now he would have to get back on the big street and ask for directions. Probably a Seattlite—they're idiots.

I circled the lot and pulled out. None of the others followed me. I guess they were too busy being embarrassed or trying to figure out who the others were. I drove home for a nap.

The next morning I was down at the courthouse bright and early to continue my search for property

connected to Mercer. After several hours I managed
to locate two more properties. The information was
coming through, but in dribs and drabs. It was
complicated by the fact that so much of it was
listed only in the name of a holding company. There
were three names that kept turning up: Sierra
Properties, Evergreenia, Inc., and The Plot, Ltd.
Two of the five pieces I'd located, 'Enry's and the
parking lot were owned by Evergreenia, or at least
they had been paying the taxes. Two more, the
West Third Avenue building and the commercial
building, were owned by The Plot, Ltd. The condominium was owned by Sierra Properties. It wasn't
much to go on. I went home, keeping an eye in my
rearview mirror but not spotting anything unusual.
When I got there, I gave Sheila a call.

"Can you talk now?" I asked when she came on
the line. "This is Scott."

"I can talk all the time," she replied, a little more
glib than usual for Sheila.

"I want some information," I told her, "about
Mercer Manor. It's about Wendell's death."

"Oh." The cheeriness disappeared. "Meet you at
the Trio—lunch?"

"Okay. See you there about noon."

"All right."

I hung up and drove around town for an hour or
so—just to exercise any pursuers who might be
around. Then I went to the Trio, a business-lunch
place downtown.

Sheila was at a table behind a little divider and
she smiled when I walked in. Lip gloss made her
mouth shine, and if you didn't sit in just the right
spot you could get caught in the glare. She was
wearing a tight green dress buttoned low to reveal
the softness of white breasts. She had a mole in the

valley between them.

"You really surprised me by calling this morning," she said, coaxing her hair into place with her fingers. "I didn't expect to hear from you again."

"I would have called you anyway," I said, probably telling the truth. "But right now I'm trying to find out something about Wendell. I'm hoping to get a clue to who killed him, or at least why."

"Oh, that's neat. I hope you can find out. I think they ought to be locked away for a hundred years." The mourning was over, and she was genuinely pissed at the people who killed Wendell, but with the same intensity she might have felt toward someone who asked her out after dating her roommate.

"I need information about all the property owned by Mercer or any of the other principals of Mercer Manor," I said. "I've been trying to locate the information through the assessor's office and I've had some luck, but not as much as I'd like." I handed her a list of the addresses I'd identified as belonging to Mercer.

She frowned, concerned. "That information is available, but I think it would be in Bud's office. I only deal with listed properties, not property the company owns. That's handled strictly by Bud."

I looked at her earnestly. "This may be important. Can you find out for me? I don't know exactly what I'm looking for, but I think that somehow these properties provided a motive for Wendell's murder."

She scowled at the list, then picked her patent-leather purse off the floor and found a place inside for the piece of paper. She looked back at me and smiled. "I'll try. I'll let you know by tomorrow."

"Okay." We had lunch and I picked up the tab. I

thought about her ass a lot as we were chatting about movies—she had seen every Clint Eastwood movie ever made. I didn't try to arrange anything though. I kept thinking about what Dr. Houston had said, that I needed love. It seemed more likely that I would get that from Deirdre, for all my reservations, than from Sheila. She sure looked good when she got up, though.

I went home, slept, and went to work without incident. The next afternoon I was sleeping when the phone rang. Before I woke I was dreaming about Sheila Woo. In my dream I had already covered her with whipped cream and I was looking around for strawberries. I got up, looking around for strawberries, when I realized the phone was ringing. I stumbled to it through the wreckage left by Chicken Man. Someday I would have to turn my talents to the domestic challenge—by then it'll be on a par with the challenge of Mount Everest.

"Forty-one," I said into the phone.

"A number?" Sheila asked. "You answer your phone with a number?"

"I was just confused," I said. I had been driving forty-one for a long time and I had thought the dispatcher was calling me.

"I got your information," she said. "I got all the stuff you wanted about when the property was bought and sold and repurchased."

Repurchased? "Can you meet me today?"

"When?"

"Anytime." Just bring your ass and the information.

"How about two-thirty at Bookworld?"

Bookworld? I was spending an inordinate amount of time in bookstores these days. I hadn't read a book since puberty unless it was on the required reading list. Bookworld was a big commercial store, unlike Gandalf's. It traded in general books, greeting cards, art supplies, and camera gear. It was your basic Woolworth's of the book business. "I'll be there," I told her.

I got there early and wandered around the aisles, tripping over little old ladies trying to find a gift for their coed niece who was into transcendental meditation and group sex. They were mostly looking at the inspirational items.

I was still wandering when I ran into Sheila. It wasn't an entirely unpleasant experience. We collided, then grabbed at one another to keep from falling over onto a bookshelf, and it was a moment before I could get myself to move my hand off her breast.

"Ooh," she said pleasantly. "This isn't the place, but maybe we could find one." She was batting her eyelashes and breathing like Donna Summers sings.

I said, "Can you get off work this afternoon?"

"I'll call in sick."

"Do. I'll meet you at your place in half an hour."

"All right." We started out of the store arm in arm.

"Do you have any whipped cream at home?" I asked her.

Sheila was no disappointment. She did everything for me that I wanted and more. I did everything I could think of in return. When we were pretty well exhausted and lying on the rug in her front room, it occurred to me she also had some information I wanted. I lay there studying her ceiling as I smoked a cigarette and fantasized future

encounters while she searched through her briefcase for the paperwork. We were both still naked,
and every time I looked at her I thought of doing it
all over again. At my age I guess everything is limited except imagination.

She crawled over to me from where her purse
had been thrown along with half her clothes. She
carried a large sheaf of photocopies. When we were
settled comfortably, the papers on my stomach and
her hip leaning against mine, she thumbed through
them and pulled out a document for me to look at.
I studied it. It was a form similar to the ones I had
been collecting from the assessor's office—bound-
ary data on a property, along with some history.
From the address I connected it to the parking lot
downtown. I studied it for a moment, looked through
the next, then the next, then the next. She had
collected information on about fifteen properties,
including the ones I had located on my own. Finally
I gathered them together and neatened the pile.
"More of the same," I said. "I see more property
now, but I still don't see anything that gives me any
reason for murder."

"There was something I thought was unusual,"
Sheila volunteered.

"What was that?"

"Well, didn't you notice that these properties
were resold several times, but really they were in
the hands of the same people?"

"Say that again."

"Well, take this one, it was purchased in 1966
when it was the Mint Hotel." I remembered that
place, a slum house for down-and-outers. "It had
been purchased for a few thousand dollars according to this record. It sold in 1967 for $40,000 and
then was sold again in 1969 for $140,000. There

was no record of it having changed hands since then."

"So? I don't get it," I said.

"Scott, all these companies are owned by the same people. The company buying is really the same as the company selling. These holding companies doing the buying and selling were run by the Mercers and Bud Baum."

I looked quickly through the remaining records. The other properties had similar histories, but with different dates. The commercial building had sold in 1971, in 1973, and again in 1975. Each time for higher prices. No record since then. 'Enry's, or rather the property on which it was located, had been purchased in 1970, sold in 1973, and again in 1977. The condominium property had been purchased in 1967, sold in 1971, then again two years later. The apartment building on West Third had sold in 1976 for a paltry $20,000, sold in 1977 for about $80,000, and sold in 1978 for $160,000. I couldn't see why it was going on, but I could see something was going on.

"You know, Sheila, you're really very bright."

Sheila smiled with delight. She was smoking a cigarette and had moved the papers so she could touch my stomach, circling my navel with a manicured finger. When I put the last of the records down, she looked at me. "Honestly, I still don't see what this could possibly have to do with Mr. Mercer's being shot."

"Maybe it doesn't," I said.

"I'm going to the bathroom," said Sheila. She got up and I watched that lovely rearend going away.

I started getting dressed. It was less than an hour before I had to be at work. Sheila looked disappointed when she came back and found me buckling my belt. I was wearing the corduroy suit pants, my new shoes, and a blue plaid wool shirt with my old jacket. "Leaving already, darling?" she said with a Hepburn imitation that wasn't all that bad.

"Have to go to work, kiddo. I'll give you a call tomorrow."

"I'll be home after six," she said. "I'd rather you didn't call me at work, what with the situation and all."

"Okay." I gathered up my papers in a stack along with the original list of addresses and descriptions. I kissed her, touched a breast and her behind, and left. I was going to be dead tonight, but it had been well worth it.

The evening went slowly and depressingly. My fares were worse than usual. I had one drunk get out of the cab in Peaceful Valley, walk up to the side of the car, and piss on the tires. Another guy took me on a half-hour shopping tour during which I had to push his cart around the store while he filled it up entirely with drinkables, including a case of beer and a few big jugs of Mad Dog 20-20.

I was pleasantly relieved when I pulled up to the Purple Onion and there waiting for me were Poet Bob and a lady friend. She was probably a few years younger than him, but just as dissipated, wearing a dress that looked like it had been made to cover a sofa. She had wrinkles on wrinkles and dyed auburn hair, the artificial color of which had tinted her skin a little at the hairline. She was a pretty classy broad for Poet Bob. She even had a little sequined evening purse, which had probably been left in a low-class dive by Mae West. They got in and Poet Bob gave me the destination—Hillyard. He had his customary duffel bag, but it seemed a little more full. He said they had fallen in love and were going to Montana.

When they got out—that took a couple of minutes—Poet Bob paid me and said, "My boy, you'll always be welcome at our place in Big Fork."

I thanked him, shook his hand, and left the two of them standing there, looking like two refugees from the sleazier side of the Depression.

My next call I could have done without—it was the special at Spooner's again. There was my curly-headed lawyer playboy about to help me reenact our Prince and the Pauper routine. I wondered if he was gay, or if he just took pleasure in giving me a bad time. Either way I was getting damn tired of it. I told him as much on our way to the apartment house in Browne's Addition. He laughed like he had heard nothing so funny since people had stopped telling Polish jokes.

"Don't worry, Moody," he told me as he climbed out of the car and overtipped me again. "I won't bother you much longer." He staggered off to his apartment house to study his briefs. I would have to watch out, working for lawyers, if this guy was typical.

I got home, had my coffee, and went to bed. I had trouble getting to sleep because the morning show was a rerun of an interview on aging with Will Geer. He had since died. It was depressing to hear him talk about vim and vigor when he was all out of it.

I finally nodded off, dreaming I was John-Boy. I was imparting wonderful insights about life to the rest of the Walton clan when Mary Ellen said I had a phone call.

"Hello, hello," I said, holding my hand up to my ear. The phone in the other room was ringing, and I soon realized I had not yet reached it in this dimension. I had to get out of bed and scramble to get it.

"Walton's Mountain," I said feebly.

"Scott? Are you all right?"

"Oh, hi, Deirdre. Yeah, I'm all right."

"Do you want to come over today?"

I thought about it. Sheila Woo wiggled across my mind. "Not today," I said. "I'm too damn tired and I have to work tonight."

"Have you thought about my offer?"

"I'm still thinking about it."

"Oh," she said, disappointment registering six on her Richter scale.

"I'll talk to you tomorrow, okay? I'll probably drop by. It's just that it's pretty hard taking time out during the work week."

"It would be more fun than what you do now, and probably easier."

Anything would be easier. "I'll think on it."

"Okay. I'll miss you."

"Me too." I always missed me. I hung up.

I dragged me back to bed and tried to get back into the dream on Walton's Mountain. That was a pleasant place to be. Instead I ended up in the hot place, a big hotel or mountain lodge that was being burned to the ground by its former owner, some guy known as the Captain. All the guests were inside screaming and moaning, asking for mercy. And the Captain himself was inside, but he was so evil he didn't care. When I got out of that dream I was happy to go to work.

I drove number fifty-nine around all evening. It was a car with bald tires, no radio, and no heater.

At about six-thirty, from an outside phone booth, teeth chattering from the cold April air, I called Sheila. When she answered she sounded as if she were speaking with a couple of cotton balls in her mouth.

"How ya doin', kid?" I asked.

"I can't talk to you now," she said, sounding distraught.

"Who the hell is that?" said another voice in the background. Suddenly the connection was broken. I stood there in the booth for a moment looking at the phone. It could have been a jealous lover prying into her affairs, but I didn't like the sound of it.

I went back to driving. When I was near her address, I drove by, checked out of the car, and walked up to the apartment. I knocked.

I stood there for a long time, knocking every so often and hoping for an answer. It had started raining by the time I left. I took a couple of fares, then I called the police department. The woman who took my call didn't seem too distressed even after I gave her some of the background.

"It could have been like you said," she told me. "Perhaps she has another friend and after she spoke to you they left."

She sounded used to getting calls about domestic disputes. "I'll tell you what I'll do, I'll try to make some inquiries. Do you know a relative or anyone I might call?"

I said I didn't, and she said she didn't think she could help me then. I said thanks and hung up the phone.

I drove around for a few more hours, pissed off and rained on. I wanted to know what had happened to her, if anything, and if she was all right, but there was no answer at her place. I finally settled into the comfortable notion that I was just being paranoid.

About three a.m. I got a call at the Mercer building on West Third. I seemed to be doing a lot of business there lately. The dispatcher told me we had had a lot of no-shows at that address this evening, including a special for good old forty-one, so not to expect too much. I drove by and parked, but no one came out. I walked toward the building. I didn't see anyone waiting for a cab, but like a fool I trotted up the stairs, opened the door, and went inside. "Bye, creep," someone said behind me, then hit me over the head with a grand piano.

CHAPTER SEVEN

When I woke I had the feeling that I wasn't really awake. For one thing, I was in heaven.

Naturally, I knew it wasn't really heaven, because I had been to this place before. It was bright. Bright white light. But I knew better than to "go toward the light." I knew that this was a fool's heaven. This was a heaven of harps and wings, but the harps were made of iron pyrite.

An angel appeared before me and told me I was in heaven. I told her she was full of it. The angel persisted in this assertion for a while, but I was wearing her down even as she began to show me my past life.

Even though I knew I was in a place that didn't exist, I was aware that I was vulnerable. Dreams, and this was some kind of dream, can be torturous. If you're a normal person, you live in dreams only briefly as you sleep. As an ex-madman, I was a veteran of a longer stay in the dream state—nearly a year.

And the dream I found myself in now seemed extraordinary—somehow I knew it would last—in fact, my first panic was over how to wake up. And when I didn't wake, I began to settle in for the long haul.

This was a dream like the dreams I experienced at the time I was going mad. At that time I had been suffering the loneliness of the break-up of my marriage and I had been medicating myself liberally with marijuana and hashish and psilocybin mushrooms. As I slid off the side of the world into madness, my dreams became more and more of a reality unto themselves. I found that I could will events in my dreams. When I woke, the personalities from my dreams would persist, sometimes for days. This dream was like those, and it brought back all the old terror, the fear that I would be lost in this place forever and would never return to the world of men. Even though this current dream was fairly pleasant, I knew that hell was up there around the bend. And it might be only one of many hells.

The angel I encountered at first soon faded and I found myself in the white room. It was an imaginary white room, but it was exactly like the white room in the jail where I had been taken when I went crazy. It was an isolation room. They had put me there as soon as they determined I was Looney Tunes and had kept me there for three days. In my first stay in the white room I had relived my childhood. In this long dream I repeated that experience.

The central event of my childhood had been the death of my mother when I was a toddler, about Allison's age. I viewed her as a saint, and as a child spent much of my time trying to understand why she had died and if it had been my fault. Emotionally, I tried to join her. My most common nightmare when I was seven was of a group of skeletons, like ghoulish pallbearers, carrying me to her grave and burying me with her. There was no other choice for me if I was to be with her—that's where she was.

In my dream, as in my madness, my mother had become a stern mistress. I was scolded and condemned. My father joined her, amid a cacophony of other voices from childhood. The condemnations were unending and unrelenting. I was back in a place I had hoped to avoid the rest of my life—the core of madness. It didn't look like I would ever wake up.

I had brought this on myself.

I had sought madness as part of a religious experience. It had been a comforting world at first, though occasionally sinister and unpredictable, like a friend who turns mean when he drinks. In time, and especially as I used marijuana and other drugs, this world became so much a part of my life that these people who scolded and condemned me were almost my only companions. Soon I was asking them for advice on everything, from what I should eat to how I should make a living. I had convinced myself that they were real people, though invisible, and were my only friends. Though they could be cruel, they could also be tender and loving—and certainly intimate, for they knew my every thought. After a few months I had all but abandoned the real world. I could be seen walking down streets and deserted stretches of highway talking to myself.

My next visitors were the police.

They took me away in a patrol car, booked me, put me into a blue jumpsuit, and threw me into a cell where I continued my conversations with persons from "the other side." The conversations were a bit more serious at that point—a little like the persecutorial conversations one might imagine taking place in hell. After a time the police put another prisoner in with me. Later I decided they had done that to judge if I was faking. I suspect my temporary cellmate was glad to get out of my presence and assured them that I was verifiably insane.

From the jail I was transported to a mental hospital where I spent three months wandering the halls, mad as a loon despite a high dose of Thorazine.

There, I went through many sessions of therapy, and one beating that resulted in a broken nose.

I went through my release from the hospital again. In this dream, just as in real life, most of my family shunned me. Most people in this part of the country fear madness even more than they fear flying or public speaking. I guess they felt I had failed some fundamental test. And perhaps I had.

There used to be a myth about being in prison. At the end of your term you would be given a suit and a minimal stipend to start your life anew. I don't know the truth of this, but I know that no such benefits are provided those involuntarily committed to the madhouse. When I returned to the streets I was wearing the same ratty clothes and carrying the same amount of money, a few dollars.

I also reentered the world with a somewhat altered nose and a belief that I was no longer among the living. I had joined my mother and my friend among the dead in all but the literal sense.

In time I had formulated my plan. Be a taxi driver. What better activity for scum. And become a detective—looking for demons, looking for evil. Well, I must have found evil. I had found it, and it had put me here, in this dream, wondering if I would ever wake up.

This was the world that enveloped me for several days. These weren't days in the usual sense. They were shorter in real time and longer in emotional time. They were periods during which various dreams and fantasies continued until some part of my system would shut down, putting me into total unconsciousness. Then, after some period, I would "reawaken" to a new fantasy—some new heaven or hell. When I was mad I spent several months in a world similar to this. At that time I was technically awake, but awake or sleeping, indoors or out, my environment was a place of magic and demons.

So, in a way, there was comfort in the familiarity of this insane environment. And my current real-life companions kept cropping up, though they were sometimes transmogrified to suit the purposes of hellish fantasy.

As I had been beaten in real life, I was beaten in my dream too. But in this dream my assailant was a different person. He was my occasional passenger, the young lawyer. He was laughing while he beat me, and he got in a lot more blows than I received in the real beating at the hospital. And Deirdre was watching. She thought it was funny. Like all good things, that dream episode ended, and another succeeded it.

Deirdre and Sheila were occasionally nice to me, but others were not so kind. Wendell returned from the dead. This was not pleasant, as it restored the notion that this was real—not a dream, but a message from "beyond." Wendell *was* dead, so he had a right to be around in an afterlife and he also had a right to be pissed at me. Present again was my friend who had died in Vietnam. And my mother.

I continued to tolerate the company of the spoiled lawyer who had become a regular passenger in my cab. How did he gain entrance into my dream anyway? Earlier he had beaten me up. Now in my dream I was variously driving the cab with him as my passenger, or riding in the cab with him as the driver. When I was driving was the more dangerous, because he kept lighting cigarettes and throwing them in my lap, or lighting trash in the back seat. In one episode he was naked on the rug in the living room with Deirdre, and I was somehow a prisoner, forced to watch. In another dream he was running away from me—laughing as he outdistanced me. He was always laughing, that guy. He had fun in my dreams.

Walter Egan was there, the black man whom I had been sent to evict from that building on West Third. I spent much of my dream time in that building for some reason—a reason that was almost clear to me, but not quite. I was stuck in that building, running up and down the stairways looking for a way out, or trapped deep in the bowels in some claustrophobic basement.

And once in a while Allison was there. In real life she was as cute and sweet as it was possible to be, but in the dream she was somehow even more dear. In the dream she always died, or I lost her somewhere. The times when she was in the dream were the times I felt myself trying hardest to escape. I spent most of this time trying to scream or sob, but was somehow unable to express my horror and sorrow with a real voice.

At times I dreamt that I could feel the presence of my body and my surroundings in the same way one can sometimes sense such things in a light sleep—during an afternoon nap, or in the early morning just before waking. At these times I tried hard to wake myself. I felt that I was near the surface and I would try to go all the way by getting control of my body. It was as if I were a mummy wrapped in bandages, my arms tightly bound to my sides. I couldn't get my eyes to open or my arms to move. In my mind I was screaming and trying to get free. I threw my body from side to side, hoping to have some actual effect in the outside world I knew was there. Finally, after one such try, I learned I had had some effect. I had thrown myself out of a hospital bed and was halfway to the floor. Wide awake.

"Goddamnit!" I yelled as I hit the tiles.

Someone grabbed at me from behind. I broke free and came to my feet punching hard. Unfortunately, it was a doctor and I landed a punch. He stumbled backward. I tried to get my bearings and at the same time tried to close my hospital gown.

The doctor fled the room and suddenly I didn't feel so aggressive. I was dizzy and would have fallen but for the nurse who caught me and helped me to the bed. She reconnected the IV and adjusted my bedding. With the realization that I was no longer in hell, I permitted the help.

"The doctor's not happy with you," the nurse volunteered.

"I wish I could say that made him unique," I told her. "Do you know if my ex-wife and daughter know I'm here?"

"They were here a couple of hours ago. The doctor let them spend time with you even though you were still unconscious."

"How long have I been here?"

"Two days."

"What happened?"

"You don't know?"

"I don't know what I was doing before I was unconscious, but I'm sure I wasn't here. And this doesn't look like my apartment—it's too nice."

"I really shouldn't say anything," she said. She was middle-aged and matronly. "There will be someone in to talk to you shortly." There were rules to follow and she was following them.

And she left.

I didn't feel well and I was tired, but I certainly didn't feel much like sleep. I adjusted the bed to as close to a sitting position as I could and tried to evaluate my situation. My limbs all seemed pretty much intact. I had a fair growth of stubble from not shaving. And, *oooh*, the back of my head was sore as hell. I felt in that area and encountered a nest of bandages that would have made a decent home for a family of robins. I was just noticing with irritation that they had cut off a large amount of hair when an officer walked into the room. He wasn't a police officer—he looked like fire department or Coast Guard to me. Since Spokane is part of the Inland Empire, I figured the odds were fire department.

He consulted paper on a clipboard. He was tanned and in his mid forties, tall and fit. "Mr. Moody?" he inquired.

"Yeah, I'm Moody."

"We wondered if you were ever going to wake up."

"So did I."

"The nurse says you don't remember what happened."

"No, I don't. Are you with the fire department?"

"Yes. I'm an investigator. You were found unconscious at the scene of a fire. One of the tenants of the building rescued you."

"I'm remembering now. I went out to West Third on a call. I don't remember a fire. I only remember arriving. Was it a big fire?"

"Big enough. Four people were killed—including the man who rescued you."

I heard a buzzing in my ears. I was tingling all over. It was an old symptom. I consoled myself that I was conscious.

The fire official consulted his clipboard again. "The man's name was Walter Egan. Did you know him?"

I looked through my mental files. They were disheveled and moldy, and some of them were missing. Walter was there, however. He was the black man I had been sent to evict. It was little consolation that I had delayed that process. "I met him," I said.

"Your employer says you never contacted him."

I realized that my little fib to Nat about not delivering the eviction notice was causing me more trouble than I had anticipated. "I tried to do a favor," I said. I explained that Egan had persuaded me to give him a little time.

"You got along okay with him, then?" The investigator's pen was in his hand, and I now understood that this was a little more than a casual chat.

"Yeah. Do you know how the fire started?"

"We're not sure. We think arson."

"Do I need a lawyer?"

"I don't know, do you?"

"I need a doctor. I'm not feeling well."

"I'll talk to you later. I'll call the nurse." The fire

investigator left and I was glad to see him go. This was all I needed. I was an arson suspect. What did they figure? I got into an argument with Egan? That poor guy. Had I caused this?

Somebody hit me. I remembered that now and the feeling in the back of my head confirmed it.

As I waited for the nurse I realized that I was feeling something else, something that always kept me wide awake. I was seething with anger.

CHAPTER EIGHT

As I convalesced I read an account of the fire in a day-old copy of the *Spokane Voice*. Of the four people killed, two had never left their rooms. They were old people with lung problems and they probably died in their sleep. A third was found in the basement and remained unidentified. The fourth was Walter Egan.

I was in the hospital for another day. Evidently I had been more sedated than injured, but they performed a number of tests to be sure. I left the hospital with a bandage, a headache, drugs I could take for pain, and an appointment for follow-up. Andrea had wanted to accompany me home, but the release time coincided with the deadline for her newspaper, so that came first.

It was late morning when I stepped into the Spokane overcast. I had had no Thorazine for days and I felt a little crazy. I called Sheila Woo at work. They hadn't seen or heard from her. She had been missing for an entire week. The fire and disappearance of Sheila gave me concern for the safety of nearly everyone, but particularly my daughter. I called Andrea at work. She seemed harried, but she wanted to speak to me.

"I'm glad you called, Scott," she said. "We were so worried about you, and Allison's been talking about you lately. She's been telling me stories about the two of you, you know, doing things together. She misses you a lot."

"Could you arrange things with the day-care center so I could take her out tomorrow? I thought maybe I could spend the whole day with her."

"That's fine with me."

"Okay. I'll pick her up in the morning."

"Are you sure you're okay?"

"Yes, I'm sure," I lied. I hung up. I called in to the dispatcher and told him I'd be coming back to work soon, but not for a couple of nights.

"Why don't you just take a vacation, Moody?" he said, and hung up the phone. Being in the hospital, personal problems, these weren't much of a reason for missing your shift in the cab.

I picked Allison up from the day-care center the next morning, then stayed with her all day, just to see that she was all right and everything was okay with her. We fed ducks in the park and went to a playground, then we went home to play with her toys. The key was under the mat where Andrea always left it. When Andrea got home I had supper with them, then Allison and I watched *The Wizard of Oz,* which happened to be on television that night.

She got scared and didn't want to watch it until I explained that right now things didn't look good for Dorothy, the Tin Man, the Scarecrow, and the Lion, but that in a little while everybody would be happy again. She still sat right next to me, her gray eyes glued to the screen until the story started moving toward a happy ending. Afterward I asked her what had scared her most.

"Fire," she said. "They were going to burn the scarecrow."

"Fire is dangerous," I told her. "You have to be awfully careful."

"I don't play with fire," she said.

"That's good," I replied.

After the movie I stayed with Allison until it was her bedtime. Andrea kept to herself, reading and doing chores, so that Allison and I could be alone. When Allison was ready for bed I gave her a hug and we kissed one another and I lifted her into the crib. I told her I would be leaving, but I would be back to see her in a few days.

"Daddy," she said.

"Yes, honey?" I looked at her eyes, but they were staring at a button on my shirt. She was playing with the button, trying to unbutton it.

"I wish you lived with me and Mommy and Bob."

"Who's Bob?"

"Mommy's boyfriend."

"Oh. Well, I wish I lived with you too, honey. But I'll be seeing you again soon. I won't be away as long this time."

"Come back tomorrow, Daddy."

"How about if I come back day after tomorrow?"

She was silent, standing on the mattress in her cotton pajamas, looking down.

"Daddy."

"Yes?"

"You have a funny nose."

"I know, honey. I got hit by a lion one time."

"A big lion?"

"Yes. He was big and mean and ferocious. But we're friends now."

She smiled. "Are you fibbing, Daddy?"

"A little." I kissed her forehead. "Good night, Punkin. I'll see you soon."

"Good night, Daddy." She lay down and I covered her up.

"How's Allison?" asked Andrea when I returned to the living room .

"Fine. Beautiful." I touched Andrea on the shoulder. "Andrea, could you give me a hug? I think I need one now."

She didn't answer, just embraced me. We stood there for a long time hanging on.

"Thanks, Andrea," I said afterward. "I'm going to go now. I'll see you."

"Scott, are you all right?" It wasn't really a question. She knew I wasn't all right. She was a little irritated with me. I could tell because she had been irritated with me before.

"I'm fine."

"What do you think would happen to Allison if something happened to you?"

I was feeling more than the usual self-pity. "It might be the best thing."

"For her or for you? Who would she depend upon?"

"What about Bob?"

"Yeah, maybe it would be Bob. He's an adult at least. I never say much about this to you, Scott, but there's something you need to realize—your mother is dead. Your friend is dead. You can't help them and you aren't responsible. But Allison is still alive. Your duty is to her."

She pushed gently on my back, herding me through the front door. Then she closed it behind me and locked it. I stood at the door for a moment, then found my way to the tree in the yard, leaned against it, and sobbed.

The next morning I made the rounds of various fire stations in the areas of all the property I had been investigating. I might not be able to help Walter Egan and I might not be able to help Wendell Mercer, but I just might be able to figure out what the hell was going on, and I might find out what had happened to Sheila.

At the fire stations, I checked their records to find out if and when there had been a fire at any of the Mercer addresses. I learned what I had expected. Many of the properties had had a serious fire at one time or another in the past ten years. The fires had occurred within months of the property changing hands. Arson was probable in all the cases, but for the most part the fire department had suspected kids or people who lived in the buildings.

All burned structures had been razed. New buildings or parking lots replaced them.

The disturbing thing was that several people had died in these fires. No wonder, if he had been involved in this, Mercer had gone through periods of depression. But he must have had partners in this endeavor. What about Baum? What of Deirdre? And were there others?

I called around until I found the arson investigator who had spoken to me in the hospital. I asked for an appointment with him.

"You were on my list anyway," he said. "How about one hour, my office."

An hour later, sitting at a chair across from his desk I asked him to explain arson to me—how it worked.

"What do you mean, how does it work?" He was sitting at a small metal desk in a third floor room of a city building downtown. He was wearing the white military shirt of the fire department upper echelon. "It works lots of ways—kerosene, gasoline, newspaper, cardboard boxes. You already know something about arson. You were in a fire." He still was looking at me as a suspect, and he wasn't too interested in me being the one asking questions.

But I persisted. "I mean arson for profit. Something really organized. How do people get it to work in their favor, and how do they get away with it?"

The man chewed on this for a minute. "We don't have much of that kind of thing in Spokane, Mr. Moody. I wonder why you want to know about this."

"I can't tell you much," I said. "It has to do with an investigation I'm conducting."

"We have the occasional case of an individual business owner who's having difficulty and decides fire is a way to recoup his losses, but that's about it."

"No, this isn't that sort of thing. I'm more interested in the type of thing where people set out to buy property with arson in mind from the beginning."

"You think that's what happened in this case? It's unlikely. That happens in places with a more run-down core—Chicago, say. Someone will buy a piece of property that is almost worthless. Usually this is slum property or something like that. They'll get it for a few thousand dollars, then they'll sell it to a fellow conspirator, usually at an inflated rate. They allow some time to pass so that it appears the market has changed, and then the original purchaser, or his agent, will buy it back again, at a higher price." The investigator leaned back in his chair and looked down at his feet as he spoke. He appeared to be a little bored with the explanation he was giving. "Let's say they bought the building for the paltry sum of eight thousand dollars and this latest sale was for ninety-five thousand dollars. In actuality no money has changed hands, but on paper the value of the building has increased ten times. Do you begin to see how the profit is involved?"

"Insurance?"

"Right. They may even have to bribe an inspector, but somehow they get the building insured for the higher amount. When it burns that's what they get for it, or nearly that amount. Afterward they have enough money to clean up the property and make a down payment on capital for development. It's a very neat scheme when it works, and arson is hard to prove, so the principals are usually safe.

"It's more prevalent, however, in some of the large cities with huge slums. That's where you find cheap properties. And it helps a great deal if you can find corrupt officials—and insurance agents."

"What would you say if I told you I think such a scheme is operating here, on a smaller scale?"

"If you get solid information, I'd like to see it." He wasn't really considering it. I think he thought I was looking for a way to redirect suspicion.

"What bothers me, Mr. Moody, is what you were doing at that fire."

"You know who I am. I drive cab. I was called by the dispatcher."

"You could have made the phone call that resulted in your being sent."

"You could check," I said.

"You overestimate us. The call was probably made from a pay phone. Calls like that can't be traced."

"Oh."

"You actually think the owners of the building were involved in some way?" he asked.

"Yes. And I think it is in some way connected to the murder of Wendell Mercer."

"You found him, didn't you?"

"Yes, I did."

"You know, Mr. Moody, we've done a preliminary evaluation of the fire and it was arson, but we've also looked at the insurance angle and it doesn't look at all unusual at this point. It's not overinsured—at least not by much."

"Not according to the current price—but that's really inflated over just a few years ago."

"Maybe. We can revisit the issue. But I have to tell you, we have some questions we would like to ask you."

"I see."

"I'd like to arrange for you to come in for some interviews. You can bring an attorney if you desire."

"Okay."

"Here's my card," he said.

I took it. "Thanks."

"Have you ever been to the scene of a fire in which someone died?"

"No."

"You know what it's like?"

"No."

"It smells like a barbecue," he said.

I said nothing.

"I'll be calling you soon, Moody. Nice to see you again."

I walked out of the office feeling a darkness come in around me. I had had enough and I figured I'd better call Garcia. I would let him pursue the leads I had developed. Even Garcia was more sympathetic than the arson invesigator. He might also help me put more pressure on the investigation to find Sheila.

"Lt. Garcia is out of the office for the day," the clerk droned. "He'll be back tomorrow."

"Thanks." For nothing. I hung up the phone. I could turn the case over to someone else, but to whom? Bleaker? I didn't like the idea of turning this information over to just anyone. All those detective novels I'd read had left me paranoid. What if someone was bought off or was willing to sell? If anyone looked bought, it was Bleaker. I would have to wait, but even one day seemed one day too long for me. For now I thought it important to ask Deirdre some questions.

I called without giving her a clue to what was on my mind and arranged a meeting for later in the day, a couple of hours before I went to work. I gathered all my information in a manila envelope and clipped the reporter's business card to it—I had found the card covered in the dirt from my now-defunct philodendron. Ralph Waldo. I knew I had heard the name somewhere when I read his story about the Mercer case. He was my young blond visitor of a week or so earlier. If I couldn't turn this stuff over to Garcia, a reporter like Waldo would find it interesting. I had been a reporter just long enough to trust newspapers more than I did politicians and bureaucrats, and by the time the story came out in the morning edition I would be safe—maybe.

I drove to Deirdre's by a roundabout route, watching the rearview mirror. I spotted no one behind me, but that didn't mean much. I knew nothing about surveillance that I had not read in a textbook.

I got to the house at four, parked the car, and went to the door with the documents.

Deirdre smiled when she admitted me. She was dressed casually in jeans and a sweater. Her hair flowed onto her shoulders, blond and glistening like in a shampoo ad.

"You've decided to take the job," she said.

"How did you figure that?"

She closed the door. "I knew something was up from the sound of your voice. This isn't just a visit. You have news or something. I guessed you were going to take the job I offered. Right?"

I shook my head. I hated to disappoint her with the news I had. "I'm still thinking about the job. I have some questions to ask about property owned by Mercer Manor, Inc."

She frowned. "I could use a drink," she said and walked around me into the living room. When I got there she was pouring Scotch into two glasses at the bar. The fireplace was lit, burning quietly, a perfect touch on a cold, overcast May afternoon.

"What business is it of yours what property is owned by Mercer Manor?" She had a challenging tone in her voice. I could see she wouldn't be an easy boss.

"Just curiosity," I told her, settling on the couch with my drink. "After I get beat up a couple of times and then someone tries to kill me I get curious."

"I don't understand what you mean."

"Do you remember the night I got attacked on your front porch?"

"Yes. He was a mugger. That happens, even in the best of neighborhoods."

"He didn't take anything from me and he seemed pretty familiar with your property. But you don't know anything about that."

"No, I don't. That was weeks ago and nothing else has happened." She curled up in the chair by the fireplace, swallowed half her drink, brought it down and held it in her hands, looking at me with glazed eyes.

"That depends on your definition of a happening. I mean, your husband was killed a few days ago—we can't be sure that guy wasn't involved. But, even discounting that, a few nights ago I got hit over the head and left in a burning building. The guy didn't manage to get me, but he killed a few other people."

"You mean the fire Monday night?"

"The fire Monday night—that was the one."

"I don't understand what this has to do with me or the business. What would anyone want from you? Why would they try to hurt you?"

"That's what I want to find out. I suspect it has to do with this." I held up my envelope full of documents.

"What's that?"

"Records," I said. "Records of transactions to buy and sell buildings. Records of fires and insurance payoffs—all of them carried on in the names of holding companies that belong to Mercer Manor, Inc., or its principals."

She seemed puzzled. "I don't understand. You act as though you're making an accusation or something, but I don't know what it is. I don't know anything about any fires. Is this something Wendell did? Or Bud?"

"It looks like they were involved. It seems to me to work like this. You have a new business, say back in the late 1960s, but you're not willing or don't have the capital to make your money in the long haul—honestly. Instead, you buy buildings with the idea in mind that you'll raise their paper value by buying and selling them a few times, then they'll conveniently burn to the ground. Maybe you have partners in the insurance business. Out of this you get ready cash to develop with, to get loans with, to play with. Pretty soon you're solvent and out of the red and you've paid back your creditors. Then you can go looking for a fancy house all your own."

"I wish you wouldn't keep putting so many 'yous' in your speech," Deirdre complained. "I didn't have anything to do with it, whatever went on." She put her drink down and held out her hand. "Let me see that. I want to look at it."

Instead of handing her the documents, I took them out and spread them on the table. She studied them with me and I showed her the correlations in dates of purchase, repurchase, and fires. After a while she was just shaking her head in disbelief.

"I must have driven him too hard," she said. "I wanted things too much. But you'll notice that my name isn't on any of the papers. I didn't know anything about this. Look as hard as you want and you won't find my name on any of this. I haven't worked in the business for years, and even then I never handled this kind of thing. I was a salesperson."

I lit one of her Salems. "You're right," I told her. "I didn't find your name on anything. But I had to hear it from you."

She nodded.

"And I want you to know what I'm going to do with these papers," I said. "I'm turning them over to the newspapers. I want them to be public knowledge or I won't be safe." I didn't bother to explain that I hoped it might help Sheila Woo. If Sheila knew the people involved, they might be holding her for what she knew. If the information was public, they'd have no reason to hold her.

"But I'll be smeared by it," Deirdre said.

"There will be suspicions. I can't help that. I don't want it, but I think in the long run it will come out that you were an innocent bystander in all this. I've got to get the information out there—I'm not going it alone. Someone—and I do suspect good old Bud—is trying to kill me."

"I can't believe that of Bud. He's always been so kind and competent. This can't really be happening. Maybe someone else attacked you the other night."

"It may not have been Bud who attacked me, but it was probably someone who works for him. There's no one else to profit by it." I gathered up the papers and stuffed them back into the envelope. Deirdre got up slowly and wandered back to the bar. She poured herself a second drink without offering me one. I stood, the envelope gripped under my arm.

"I'm going to take off now. I'll call you tomorrow. I'm sorry about all this, but believe me, if it could be avoided, I'd avoid it."

Deirdre came over to me, looking like someone who's been ill for a long time. She put her arms around my waist and rested her head against my chest. "Scott, just don't think I'm involved in any of this. I don't want you to think that of me. I need your respect too much."

Now I felt sorry for her, for the things I had believed. I put my free arm around her, pressed my face into her hair. "It'll be okay. I'll be around and the storm will blow over before long."

"I hope you're right. What are you going to do now?"

"I'm going to work. Then I'm going to visit a friend of mine at the newspaper office. By morning all this will be over." She held her head up and I kissed her. Then I left, breaking free of her arms gently and reluctantly. As I walked out she was returning to the bar.

I drove away. There was a car some ways behind me, but after a while it turned off and I breathed easier. I had a hamburger for dinner, then drove out to the cab lot. It was getting dark and I knew I was late, but I wasn't worried about that. I wanted the cover of darkness. Anyone following me would think I was just going to work, not to the police or the newspapers. It might give me a few hours breathing time.

The dispatcher assigned me number forty-one, but when I went to get it, it was being filled with gas at the lot pumps. The Laughing Skeleton was in line to have his car filled up too, so he got out to shoot the shit. The Laughing Skeleton was six-feet-three and weighed 130 pounds. He was always telling corny jokes, then laughing his head off before he finished the punch line. He was a good guy even though he had a pee-H-dee in English literature. He lounged easily beside me under the lights of the cab lot by the open gate. The cranky old mechanic who had been with the company for years was pumping the gas.

"Do you know how to tell if a woman is wearing underpants?" he asked, a sly grin on his skull.

"No," I said, not caring. "How do you tell?"

"You check for dandruff on her shoes," he said, and giggled and guffawed uproariously. He sounded like a hyena in the Grand Canyon. The Laughing Skeleton lurched forward in his laughter and threw his arm around my shoulder for support. He was still laughing when the hilarity was interrupted by a sharp cracking noise from the empty field across from the cab lot. The Laughing Skeleton wheezed a little in his laughter and crumpled. We both hit the ground at about the same time. The only thing I had learned about combat was always to do it lying down. I had not felt this way since Vietnam—being in a compound with the lights on and someone out there in the darkness with a gun.

The silence was broken suddenly by a car accelerating. It sounded like a sports car, but it was hard to tell because another vehicle noise was interfering. Out of the darkness Julia Baldwin's old pickup truck zoomed by the cab lot, bouncing in the potholes of the poorly maintained road. What the hell was going on? I crawled over to the Laughing Skeleton.

"Man, I could use a joint," he breathed. There was a bright red spot on his shirt on the right side. "This hurts like hell. I can't breathe very well."

His eyes were fluttering and he was wheezing when he breathed. I looked under his shirt and saw a tiny hole in his chest. He had been hit in the lung, probably by a small caliber bullet.

"I'll get an ambulance," I told him, as reassuringly as I could, and I jumped up and ran for the cab office.

"What the hell's going on out there?" the dispatcher asked me when I got inside.

"Someone shot the Laughing Skeleton!" I said. "We need to get an ambulance, then call the police. I'd like to get out of here before they arrive, though. In the meantime I don't think you ought to come outside."

The dispatcher calmly punched the number for the aid car. He turned to me again between taking calls and telling cabs where to go. "Who the hell shot him?" he asked.

"I don't know, but I think whoever did it is gone now. I want to get out and take a few calls before I spend half my life in the police station being asked questions when I don't have any answers."

"Okay. Just as long as the aid car gets here before the police do, because I want you to help."

"I'm going out to see how he's doing." I grabbed the wool army blanket off the day cot in the corner of the room and took the pillow with it.

"Hey, that's *my* pillow," the dispatcher protested.

"I'll have it right back," I said. I went outside.

The Laughing Skeleton was in the same place as before, but now there was a joint between his lips. Our garage mechanic was standing nearby looking at the Laughing Skeleton with what appeared to be casual curiosity, just wondering if he would die.

I spread a blanket over him, propped his feet up with the pillow. I watched the glow at the tip of the joint brighten.

"Man, you shouldn't be doing that," I said. "I think you've been hit in the lung." I reached toward the joint to take it away, but the Laughing Skeleton moved his head to the side.

"No way, José. It helps. What you could do is

take the lid and some rolled joints out of my pocket because they'll find it."

I did as instructed and by then the ambulance arrived. At the first sign of the aid car I headed toward cab forty-one, planning to get out of the area.

"We've got some weird citizens in this city if they're picking off cab drivers at the lot," said the mechanic as I climbed into the cab.

"We sure do," I said. I signed in with the dispatcher, but this time I told him I was going to run an errand before I took a cab stand. I told him it was a favor for the Laughing Skeleton. He said, "We protect our own. Take care of it. How long you going to be?"

"An hour, I hope, but maybe a bit more."

"Okay."

I headed into town. I watched for anyone following, but there was so much traffic it was hard to keep track of any one set of headlights. I hoped the suspense would soon be over. When the story was in the hands of the reporter, that should be the end of it.

The closest parking spot I could find was a block from the newspaper office. I spun the car into the curb, hopped out, and trotted the distance. It was a quiet, cloudless night and the downtown avenue was empty except for a few people wandering around outside the hotels and bars.

I took the musty elevator to the fifth floor where the *Spokane Voice* news department was housed. I opened the double doors and walked in. No one looked up. I was in a huge, high-ceiling room full of old desks and older typewriters. A woman was sitting at a dirty desk just inside the door, typing. She was a woman of forty-five or so and looked like she had seen just about everything. She had graying black hair and wore glasses. The stub of a dead cigarette hung from the corner of her mouth.

"Can you tell me where to find Ralph Waldo?" I asked her.

She leaned over a wastebasket beside her desk and dropped the cigarette from her mouth. "How the fuck would I know?" she asked without looking up. "I'm just the arts editor here. I don't have a fucking thing to do with his department."

"Beg pardon," I said and walked over to a kid pounding a keyboard. "Ralph Waldo," I said, "could you tell me where to find him?"

The kid was no more than twenty. He had black hair and a thin face of the kind given to the protagonists of English literary novels—the type where the main character contracts tuberculosis near the end of the book, just as he is about to succeed. "Behind that pillar," he said, pointing over his shoulder. "But I think he's pretty busy."

"Thanks."

Waldo was slouched in his chair, smoking a cigarette and reading *Trouble Is My Business*. At least we had similar tastes in literature. He glanced up as I rounded the pillar, then gave me a second look. He dropped the book into a desk drawer.

"Imagine that," he said acidly, "you dropping by my office after leaving me to be mugged on your doorstep. Do you know I'm paying for that camera out of my own wages?"

"Hey. I told you that's how they'd handle it," I said. "I used to work for a cheap newspaper." I tossed the records, still in the manila envelope, onto his desk. "But I think I can make it up to you. Here's the rest of the story on Wendell Mercer's murder, and I can give you more details about his disappearance. All I want is to make sure that the people who lived with him are cleared. And I need the story to hit the streets in the morning."

Waldo picked up the envelope with his slim hands, opened it, and studied it with brown eyes that got wider as he sifted through the documents. When he had been through them once and was going through them again, he said, "But what does all this mean?"

I rolled my eyes skyward. Jesus. "It means that the owners of Mercer Manor, Inc. are running an arson ring," I told him. "I suspect, though I do not have absolute proof, that Mercer was killed because of it. I don't know exactly why, but perhaps he was backing out or he was going to go to the police with it. I think he was through with the scheme."

"Does anyone else know about this?" I could see a fanatical zeal coming to his eyes. He could taste this story, see it being picked up by *The Washington Post.*

"No one," I assured him, "though the police will know about it by tomorrow. Those documents are only for you to make copies. I want to hold onto them."

"I'll have to see my editor," he murmured, still studying the documents. "Just a minute." He got up and headed across the vast room.

I borrowed one of his cigarettes, lit it, and drank in the familar sights and smells of a newsroom. I was almost nauseous from the experience by the time he returned.

"He wants to talk to you," Waldo said.

"Okay." I followed him through the newsroom to the office of the managing editor.

Waldo knocked and a deep voice from within said, "Enter."

We walked into an office decorated sometime during the Great Depression. Everything was brown or black except for the rug and the editor. The rug was green.

The editor, a man in his late fifties, was balding and wrinkled and wore a pair of half-glasses set low on his nose. A stubby cigar jutted from a corner of his mouth. He was leaning back in his chair in his shirt sleeves—a white shirt of course—with his tie loosened, and he was holding something in his chubby hands, something which connected the two hands at the center of his expansive stomach. When I got closer I could see that it was a paper clip, held carefully by the stubby finger and thumb of each hand.

"This is Scott Moody, Mr. Curtis. Moody, my editor, Reginald Curtis."

Curtis didn't move, just nodded at the introduction. He fiddled with his paper clip and chewed his cigar, waiting for my spiel.

I explained how I got into the case, trying to make cabbing look secondary to my investigative work. That wasn't easy. He listened to me stoically, bending the paper clip with his fingers until toward the end of the story the paper clip broke and he tossed it into the wastebasket.

"You know why I'm still a little leery of this story?" he asked when I had finished.

"No, I don't."

"I don't know who the hell you are."

"Mr. Curtis, this is the private investigator who brought Wendell Mercer in," said Waldo with the universal exasperation experienced by people trying to explain something to a manager. "I think he knows what he's talking about."

"Well, it'll be your ass if he doesn't. The documents look all right. We'll use them without all the dramatics about attempts on his life. In fact, if you can leave him out of the story, do it."

"Thanks," I said. "That's what I want."

Curtis looked at me curiously. "Oh yeah? I thought you were a hungry private investigator looking for publicity. In that case, Waldo, use his name."

This was one place I wouldn't ever work.

Waldo made copies and assured me the story would be out in the morning. He interviewed me again and I gave him all the details I could. By the time I left, I was whistling. The next morning I would be able to walk into Garcia's office and fill him in. Then, possibly, we could try to find Sheila.

CHAPTER NINE

The next day was a heavier-than-usual news day. I picked up the *Spokane Voice* around dawn during a coffee break and looked through the arson story. As the editor had promised, my name was mentioned prominently throughout, and so, of course, were the names of Bud Baum and the late Wendell Mercer. I was happy with the story in the *Voice* and things would have been just fine except for the stories in the other daily papers. I picked them up at seven-thirty, just before I was coming off shift. They didn't have the arson story, but they had some other stories of interest that had been added to the front page, shoving some national and feature news to the back sections. One of the stories was about one of the biggest drug busts in

Spokane history. Those arrested included one Julia Baldwin. With her were a number of others ranging in age from twenty-five to forty. I assumed this included Chicken Man and Julia's other cohorts. I did learn from the story the identity of the black girl I had seen the other night—Adella Villa. She was Cuban and had apparently been involved in the transport of drugs from Florida to the Northwest.

That would probably be a nice drive—through New Mexico possibly.

They had all been arrested at a seamy address down in Peaceful Valley, a community which, despite its location in a beautiful area near the river, was somewhat disreputable. With all the money they had from drugs you'd think they could have afforded something a little more comfortable.

All had been booked on drug charges and an investigation was underway to see if there was a connection between drugs and Mercer's death.

This didn't seem right to me. My theory was that Mercer was killed by Bud—or someone Bud hired. I didn't know him well, but Bud was the only likely co-conspirator with Mercer, and therefore the only guy with a motive—not to mention he was sweet on Mercer's wife.

There was evidence to support my theory—if you read it my way. It was in a sidebar near the main story. The headline read: **Realtor Commits Suicide**. Bud Baum had been discovered—probably by some reporter out to verify facts from my story—at three a.m. He was dead of a gunshot wound. Signs indicated he had shot himself in the head with the .22 caliber pistol found beside his body. An autopsy and police investigation were planned.

But my theory had problems. It was possible that Bud was the kind of guy who just fell apart at the slightest sign that his crimes were going to become public, but he didn't seem the type to me. And he was dead before this news came out. I was worried that someone else was still at large—someone who knew Bud and maybe killed him.

Still, most of this news, somber as it was, had a calming effect on me. I sat in Casey's diner with coffee and a danish, feeling smug and relieved. I was free of this at last. I could go back to a normal routine.

Except, of course, for a minor detail—and that was in the newspaper too. It was an eighteen-point headline on page twenty-four that read: **Family Reports Woman Missing**.

Sheila Woo was still gone. The legal corralling of the 1313 Olympus gang and the ostensible guilt of one very defunct Bud Baum could not change that fact, though I called her number just in case she had returned. A man answered the phone and wanted to know who was calling.

"A friend of hers," I said, noncommittally. "I heard she was missing. She hasn't returned, eh?"

"Who is this?" the man asked again, and I hung up. It could have been her father, or it could have been the police, but whoever it was, I didn't want to talk to them. I would have to look into her disappearance without becoming a possible suspect in yet another crime.

I would start my search by visiting Deirdre. I wanted to show her the newspaper. This was partly to break the news to her, but I also wanted to see her reaction. She was still too close to this to remain unsuspected.

Her newspaper was still on the stoop when I arrived. I picked it up and rang the doorbell.

"Who is it?" a sleepy voice asked from the other

side of the door.

"Scott," I said. I looked around the neighbor-hood. It was a quiet place at this time of the morning. A light mist drifted over the street and the expensive landscapes of the neighborhood. Colors blended together in the grayness of God's very indirect lighting. The only color that stood out was the bright red of a BMW parked across the street.

"You're so early," said Deirdre as she opened the door. "Come on in." Even with sleep-swollen eyes she looked good to me. I didn't want to give her the news, but I knew I had to. It would mean scandal whether she wanted it or not. We sat in the living room and I told her about it. She seemed shocked and a little concerned.

"Poor Bud," she said. "He was never my favorite, but he was a friend. I'm so sorry for him." She paused, then continued, "They aren't going to get me into this, are they?"

"I doubt it. I think you're in the clear."

"You're sure?"

"As I can be. You'd know better than I."

She licked her lips, ran nervous fingers over them. "No, I'm okay. I'm all right." She thought a minute, then said, "A lot of our money came from this scheme, then?" It was something she knew, and yet she was asking.

"A lot of it."

"I don't want to think about it." She leaned against me and gripped my arms with both her hands. "Poor Wendell. He must have been tortured by it."

"And he was finally killed when he wanted out," I said.

"Stay for a while," she said. "I need you."

Something was bothering me, but it wasn't as

strong as my attraction to Deirdre. I held her and we kissed. If it hadn't been for a rude habit I have of opening my eyes, I wouldn't have noticed the blur of movement at the window at the side of the house. It was just a flicker of dark brown hair. I pulled back from Deirdre, looking in that direction. I looked at her. She was very tense. I saw another movement, this time heading for the street, fast. I exchanged glances with Deirdre.

"It's my brother," she said quickly.

"He's a hell of a jogger," I said, and sprinted for the door. I scrambled out onto the porch as the red BMW roared twice, winding up, then shot out of its parking spot and fled down the street. If I had been a bit faster I could have caught up with it in time to be run over. As it was, I emerged from between two parked cars just as a Cadillac was passing through the neighborhood. The man in the car yelled at me as the sound of the BMW receded.

Pictures were coming together in my head—the BMW, the curly hair of my law student passenger. I had seen him clearly enough as the car took off to recognize my friend, a young man who at the age of twenty-eight or twenty-nine was about right to keep a lonely woman entertained.

Deirdre was on the porch. She was not smiling, but that was only through great effort at composure.

"Who was he?" I asked, as impolitely as possible. "He had something to do with this. He was no late entry."

"I don't know," she said. "He must have been prowling the neighborhood."

"A minute ago he was your brother."

"A minute ago I thought you might catch up with him. You can leave anytime you want, Scott."

"Sure. As soon as I make a call." I walked past her into the house and called the Public Safety Building. Garcia was in, but he was not enthused to hear from me.

"Get me a name," he said. "So far all you're telling me is that Mrs. Mercer has a friend, but I'll talk to him if you get me a name and an address. By the way, when you get a chance, I'd like you to come in. I have a few questions for you."

I hung up the phone. Deirdre stood fuming nearby. "Get out," she said.

I looked at her a moment—she was staring at me with quiet anger. The glass coffee table and decanter were beside me. I grabbed the table under the edge and jerked with all my strength. It jumped into the air and smashed on the rug, scattering booze and crystal across the room.

"I'll report you to the police," she said.

"What was a nice guy like me doing in a girl like you?" I asked, and left the house.

The phone rang about ten o'clock. When it sounded I was dreaming. In my dream I was in a big cage, full of gorillas.

Gorillas. Gorillas scooting all over the place in office chairs. It was like bumper cars except with a bunch of gorillas. Pretty fun.

I rose from bed to answer the phone. As I looked around I saw there were no gorillas in office chairs.

It was Nat Goodie and he was mad as hell.

"You won't get any more work from me," he said, right off. "You'll be lucky if you can stay out of the county jail."

"You knew about the arson, didn't you?" I challenged him. "You know the guy who's sleeping with Deirdre."

He hung up.

CHAPTER TEN

When a ballistics test was run on the pistol found beside Bud Baum's body it was confirmed as the gun that had killed Wendell Mercer. Motive, opportunity, and evidence tied Bud Baum, posthumously, to the killing.

Though I did all I could to tie Deirdre Mercer to fraud and arson, she stayed clear. The guy with the BMW was not found or identified. Deirdre denied he had even existed, which was interesting. Lieutenant Garcia called me in regularly for "conversations," which I was sure were intended to tie me to some crime, but so far he had nothing conclusive enough to charge me. Julia Baldwin and her friends were being prosecuted for selling drugs and were expected to receive harsher sentences as a result of their outspoken and unpopular politics. One member of the gang had not been arrested as I had originally presumed. Chicken Man was still free.

And Sheila Woo did not emerge from the mystery surrounding her disappearance. A couple of weeks after she was missed, her parents had a poster printed up at a job printer which was widely distributed throughout the Northwest. Every time I read about a body discovered or heard details of an autopsy, I reenacted the crime in my mind as having been carried out against dear Sheila.

I learned to hate again—I mean really hate, not just the usual disdain I felt for the world. Perhaps it was a natural part of the healing process. I thought often about the young law student who had ridden in my cab. I was quite certain that in some fashion he was responsible for Sheila's disappearance and perhaps quite a few other violent acts. I tried to trace him through the law school and through the apartment building to which I had delivered him a number of times. He told me he was a lawyer, but there was no record of him at the law school. I had thought the apartment house was his address, but no one at the apartment house had ever seen him, or at least did not respond to my description of him. I had begun canvassing other apartment houses in the vicinity without result.

But what the driver of that red BMW did not count on was my persistence, my hanging around Deirdre's house early in the morning waiting for him to show up. And neither of us had expected the involvement of a high-cholesterol, nondenominational, radical, fatty-acid known colloquially as Chicken Man. He turned out to have a romantic attachment to justice—as well as a pragmatic devotion to self-interest. It was about a month after my newspaper buddy, Ralph Waldo, was hired by *The Washington Post,* that I got a friendly phone call from the psychedelic Buddha.

"You up?" said the deep, insensitive voice.

"I'm a little depressed actually," I replied, nodding off for a moment, then waking up as my head hit the phone. I had been home from my mobile office for about two hours, in the deepest moments of Thorazine sleep, and this electronic interruption of my rest was raising hell with my very uncollected subconscious.

"Do you know who this is?"

"A caller for Christ?" I ventured.

"Chicken Man!" he said, sounding like the announcer for the old *Superman* series.

I wasn't awake yet, but now I was listening, grateful this meeting was taking place over the phone. "I'm surprised to hear from you."

"People always are," he said. "It's the way I affect people."

"Can I do anything for you? Always glad to do a favor." To keep my limbs intact.

"No, but I can do you a favor."

Uneasy, I said, "What?"

"I know the guy you're after," he told me. "He's the guy who shot that cab driver."

I remembered the sight of the old pickup with Chicken Man at the wheel, bouncing across the field next to the cab lot on the night the Laughing Skeleton had been shot. He had subsequently recovered, but he seldom stopped to b.s. with me anymore. For the first time during this conversation I felt a tiny gratitude for hearing from Chicken Man. Still, there was a little regret this information couldn't have come from someone else.

"Do you know where he lives?" I asked.

"I know a place he visits regularly," he said.

"Where?"

"I'd like you to meet me there."

"I'll call the police."

"Not if you ever want to see me you won't. I want your help in getting clear of them."

"You want your name cleared?" It seemed as unlikely he would worry about a thing like that as that Jesse James got upset when his fingernails were too long.

"Hey, I have to live here," he protested. "My folks are here. They think I'm some kind of crook or something. And look, my high school is having a reunion this year and I can't go if there's a warrant out for my arrest."

Geez. Even monsters will be human.

"So I'm supposed to meet you at this place, we catch this guy, then I can call the police?"

"And then, while I'm hiding out again, you can convince the cops that this proves I'm a really good guy, and that, besides, they don't have any evidence against me."

"I get it," I said, "But the thing is, it doesn't sound all that safe."

The next few words told me Chicken Man was getting impatient with me being some kind of prima donna pansy.

"*I'll* be there," he said, "I can handle myself. This guy doesn't have a gun anymore—that I know of."

"That you know of." Great. "Where should I meet you?" I asked.

He gave me the address, after which I couldn't entirely control my laughter.

"That," I said, about to give up on this hopeless fool and go back to sleep, "is Deirdre Mercer's address and I've been watching that house for more than a month."

"What day of the week are you off work?" he asked.

"Sunday, usually," I answered, perplexed.

"And what do you usually do?"

"Visit my daughter—why?"

"It's like you figure this guy doesn't know anything about you. Sunday is his day to see the rich bitch. Face it, Moody, nobody but you even believes this guy exists. Nobody is looking for him. He didn't even have to get rid of his car. He just drives it a little less."

It hurt my ego that the Incredible Hulk had done a better job of sleuthing than me.

"Look, I followed you for two weeks before that cabbie was shot, and I saw this guy following you. He worked for your realtor friend. Are you interested, or not?"

"What time?"

He told me ten p.m. I hung up, fell asleep, and dreamed for the rest of the day.

My dreams were remarkably violent.

I arrived earlier than ten at the appointed spot, a corner of a local park, Cliff Park, which overlooks downtown Spokane from high on the South Hill. It is a strange park, not because it is wooded or landscaped—city parks are often like that—but in that its central feature is a kind of small Devil's Tower, a column of rock which rises several stories into the air and whose summit can be reached by a stairway. The top is carpeted in landscaped grass, as smooth as a putting green. It is a very peculiar, but very beautiful park.

A block or so from this wonder, by a tree, stood a brooding Chicken Man. I was comforted that his mindset had not been basically altered during his time as a fugitive.

He didn't smile when he saw me approach, but he nodded, which was a lot friendlier than Chicken Man had ever been toward me before. I nodded in return, careful not to insult him by fawning.

"He gets here sometime between now and midnight, stays until near dawn," he said quietly. "I found a good place to watch from."

He led the way from the park down a path, across a lower road and along several streets until we had neared Deirdre's house. The spot he had chosen was a wooded area on a large estate across from Deirdre's. We sat in a comfortable but unobtrusive spot that gave us a good view of her house, the street, and, incidently, the lights of the city.

Even a nice view couldn't make the moment all that romantic.

Chicken Man, much to my delight, was not greatly given to conversation. He did, however, drop a few tidbits of information about the suspect; namely, that he had shot the Laughing Skeleton while trying to shoot me, that he had been sleeping with Deirdre long before I had, and that his name was Patrick.

He had heard him addressed by this name when Deirdre greeted him at the door one night. I remembered that name too. The name crossed off the list of Mercer employees. The name Sheila said was a former employee who could not have had anything to do with this. I wished she had not decided to protect him, and I wondered again if she was alive.

In all that Chicken Man had learned, he had never ascertained, though he had tried, where the man lived. It was evidently damned hard to follow a BMW with a 1948 Ford pickup and Chicken Man couldn't afford better. The only reason he had learned as much as he had was that Chicken Man had been following me around town and the red BMW had turned up everywhere I went.

We waited long enough that I began to feel some camaraderie with the Chicken Man. I found the stony silence a little boring, and I confess to having had a real curiosity about Chicken Man's high school reunion—curiosity about the simple fact that Chicken Man had actually gone to school. I wondered what kinds of things had been written in his yearbook, or if his friends had just scratched something in with their paws. I kept most of my friendly feelings to myself, but I did offer one observation as we sat waiting.

"I'm surprised you were able to stay in hiding," I told him.

"Don't tell anybody," he confided, "but I'm staying at my mom's house."

We sat quietly. It was shortly before midnight that I heard a car approaching, one with an energetic sound characteristic of the BMW. It pulled around a corner and wheeled into an open spot half a block away. From the way Chicken Man looked at it, and from his slow movement toward the street, I didn't have to ask if this was the right car. I followed quietly down to the row of parked cars.

The man came down the street whistling. Either this was the wrong guy, or I wanted to kill him just for his nonchalance.

Things would have gone better had Chicken Man not seen too many spy movies, because the approach he tried was a little too threatening. As the man neared us, Chicken Man wandered into the street and casually asked him for a light. He didn't bother to have a cigarette out.

I saw the man for just a second in the light of a distant street lamp, the unmistakable, intelligent, handsome, wise-ass face of my regular passenger, bon vivant, and murder suspect. Then he was sprinting up the hill away from us, and with a hell of a good chance of getting away.

Chicken Man, the guy who earlier in the day had said, "I'll be there," as though that was a guarantee of success, was of no use at all. We left him behind in the first heat. It was like bringing a tank to race at Le Mans.

I wasn't that much better. I was in a hell of a shape—thirty-five, and on heavy tranquilizers. I was dropping back when I saw him take the path to the top of Cliff Park. I didn't see why he would want to take that path. Maybe he knew another way down. I followed, cautiously, hoping against hope that Chicken Man would call the police.

Unfortunately, Patrick's only way out of that park appeared to be over my dead body, and that didn't seem as much of a barrier as I would have liked.

I had just reached the top of the narrow, landscaped mesa when he appeared before me.

"Hi, Moody," he said, smiling just a little, as always. His curly hair was longer than on our last meeting.

"Look," I told him, "I don't want trouble . . ."

But he hit me anyway, alongside the head. His hands were up and his body held a boxing stance. He tapped me again, this time on the edge of the jaw. I assumed a boxing position, or what I imagined it should be. This was an uneven match.

"Look," I said, feeling numbness in the two places he had hit. "I'm not trying to hurt you. I want you to talk to the police, that's all. I just want to know how you fit into all this."

"You do, huh, Moody?" He hit me again. "I'm just a friend of the family, Moody, that's all. I was just doing some friends a favor." He moved toward me again and I backed up. The top of the park was empty, quiet. The lawn stretched out around us, and in the background the lights of the city glowed.

"I just want to talk to you," I said. I sounded like I was begging again.

"Moody, you ain't got a chance to talk to me. You're going to be lucky to live, and I figure you ain't got much luck. I'm going to get what I want. I'm going to get the rich lady, Moody. You're not. She hates your guts, did you know that?" He hit me again, harder—and this time on the nose. "And Sheila wasn't yours either, you know that? She kept my name off that list she gave you because she's a girlfriend."

"Is she alive?"

"You know the old saying—that's for me to know and you to find out."

"You know where she is?"

He shrugged, like, *maybe I do, maybe I don't.*

The trouble with this guy was, he was a dilettante. He was so cocky that even though he knew that Chicken Man, slow as he was, was on his way, and possibly the police too, he took his ease to play with me. It was the same as when he had called my cab, just to meet me and give me a hard time. He just could not lose.

He danced toward me and slapped me on the head again, as I had not been slapped since I was a kid. I was being backed toward a rock wall and a vertical exit.

I had paid little attention, in my life, to methods of defending myself or hurting others. I learned little of it as a boy, and had scant need of it in college. What I had been taught in the army had involved tempered steel and lead and explosive powders. I had, in thirty-odd years, learned only one violent move that I could, at the moment, remember. It had been taught to me by a casual acquaintance in the early 1960s during a drunken moment at a beer kegger. It was a karate move. The first blow was a downward, knife-like stroke, with the side of the hand to the base of the opponent's nose. This move was intended to break the bone of the nose. It was to be followed by a second blow, a piston-like movement directed at the center of the nose. According to my drunken instructor, this would drive the bone up into the brain. It was the only defensive movement I knew, and I was angry enough and frightened enough to use it.

But when I started the movement I felt the old feelings, the internal forces, my demons, taking over. My movement forward was doubled in force by their action. My hand was pulled from my control, acted on its own, and struck him very hard on the bridge of the nose, hard enough that I winced at the pain to my hand. My other arm, already ordered by me to move, did so with an alarming strength that I had not invoked, even in my present fear and anger. He could not have expected this. He could not know that a schizophrenic's demons had just been turned loose on him. I didn't know they would do it, either. I was as surprised as he.

Maybe they thought he would kill us all if they didn't defend me.

My opponent blinked when I rapped him across the nose, and smiled ever so slightly, as though what I had done struck him funny. But the second blow he took more seriously. While his eyes didn't cross, as they do in cartoons and movies when someone is hit, they did seem to lose focus, as though they had been unplugged at some connection to the brain. His knees buckled and he collapsed in a heap at my feet, limbs sprawled at odd angles. It reminded me of a man I had seen minutes after he had been killed in a shootout with the Spokane police. A psychotic who had gone on a rampage. I was a passerby after the event and witnessed his death, his arms and legs splayed in weird positions, his face sallow and dead.

But Patrick wasn't dead. His nose was probably broken, and he was spilling blood. I didn't know what damage my attack had caused, probably not what my drunken instructor had intended, but Patrick was down for the count anyway.

I pinched my handkerchief on his nose and that stopped some of the blood. After a moment he came to, coughing. By some reflex, Patrick held the handkerchief on his nose and I turned him onto his side so that, if he coughed, he would be able to spit the blood out.

By the time Chicken Man arrived, Patrick had his eyes open and was mumbling a little, though without making a good deal of sense. He reminded me of one of my uncles who had become simple in his old age and who rambled in a gentle voice about events long forgotten and lost from context. But with his nose damaged, Patrick also sounded like he had a terrible cold.

Chicken Man was predictably uneasy.

"The police are coming," he said. "I didn't like it, but I called them—I thought the guy would kill you. I'm going now."

He did so. He didn't even say goodbye.

I waited with Patrick until the police and an ambulance arrived. They had quite a time getting Patrick down from Cliff Park.

Just for the hell of it, I guess, they put me into handcuffs.

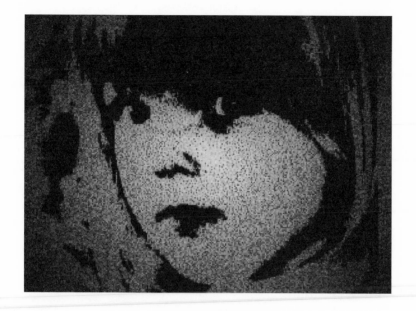

CHAPTER ELEVEN

If a person knows he's going to die, and testifies informally, says something—even to a passing bum—before he dies, it is known as a death-bed confession, or death-bed testimony, or something like that, and it will stand up in court. If he just goes into coma after such testimony, it's a little more ambiguous.

Patrick Wills was conscious when I turned him over to the police, and he was conscious long enough in the ambulance to say a lot of things, which, with a certain knowledge of the Mercer case, confirmed some of my suspicions. He said that he had worked for Bud Baum and Wendell Mercer while he was a student, that he had been a friend of Baum's. The form of payment he had received and the exact nature of the work wasn't made clear.

He said, perhaps under the spell of the drugs they were giving him, or out of some anxiety, that he had been responsible for the death of some people. I had the impression he meant Bud and Sheila and Mercer. That was about all he said before he became unconscious.

I had hoped that finding Patrick would resolve some things, help to find Sheila, and clear me of suspicion. However, from the point of view of the police, things were a little more muddled. For one thing, they had no particular reason to suspect this guy of anything. Deirdre did not confirm her acquaintance with him when they called her that night. From their point of view I was either a criminal or a nut and I had perhaps assaulted a perfectly innocent man.

I spent the rest of that night in an interrogation room and in various offices at the Public Safety Building. I continued to wear handcuffs, but I did manage to talk an officer into buying me cigarettes so I could slowly begin working on my suicide efforts, starting with smoking myself to death.

At about two a.m., Garcia showed up and asked me a few questions. He listened to my explanation, but with no particular interest.

"You've done it to yourself this time, Moody," he told me right before he left again.

I lit another cigarette and reclined on a bench in the sterile interrogation room. I would have to get used to this kind of accommodation. It looked like no matter which road I took, it led to a place like this. I could not even think about Allison, about the consequences this could have for her. I really had lost all my options. I wouldn't be free anymore. I would be in lockup—unable to do anything to clear my name, but pray.

I finally fell asleep even though I was freezing in the room and though the bench kept reminding me that wood made a poor mattress. I awakened when I fell to the floor at Garcia's feet.

"You're not that graceful, Moody," he said, and lit a cigarette. I heard the click of his lighter being shut. The interrogation room was dark except for light from the doorway. Evidently, someone had noticed me sleeping and had switched off the lights.

I crawled to my feet. That was tough with the handcuffs, and Garcia had to help me.

Casually, Garcia said, "We found your guy's house."

"He lived in a house? I thought he had an apartment." I was groggy, and thinking about as well as usual.

"He had a house. We found something there. I'd like your opinion on it."

"What did you find?"

"You'll see soon enough." He led me out of the room by my arm. We walked down the hallway a hundred feet. He opened a door and gently pushed me inside. It was Garcia's office. There was Garcia's desk, his file cabinets, a visitor's chair, and a sofa. Sitting on the sofa, wrapped in a blanket and smoking a cigarette, was Sheila Woo.

I didn't run to her, or say anything to her. I simply began crying. I don't mean that I contained a few dignified sobs, or that I cried in little spurts of emotion. I mean I bawled like a toddler in that sort of wail of emotion that is uncontrollable. Sheila ran to me and hugged me as I continued to sob, embarrassed, foolish, stupid. I knew the difference, but could not help identifying Sheila with my mother, with the fact that my mother had never come back from the dead, but Sheila had. I tried to reciprocate the affection Sheila lavished on me, but it was difficult with the handcuffs. Finally, Garcia broke in between us to unlock the cuffs so we could hug.

Garcia said, "I don't know how you got into this business, Moody, but you ought to get out of it. You're not suited for it."

With Sheila back from the dead, and with Patrick's identity known, the police came up with some hard facts and tied him to the case. Of course, a man in coma cannot be brought to trial. Therefore, a lot of questions remained unanswered.

The fire department investigation finally cleared me. They tied Patrick to acts of arson as long ago as ten years—fires that had nothing to do with the Mercers.

"He was a firebug," Garcia said when he called me in and told me the good news. "I think he got together with Mercer and Baum and turned out to be a little too talented at his work. He got a kick out of it. I think his talent for crime overwhelmed them. I don't think it was very long before the tail was wagging the dog. They were afraid of him—turns out with good reason."

"I don't understand," I said. "How could you know he was a firebug in these fires? Some of them happened a long time ago."

"He was questioned about some arson fires in the early 1970s. He was a person of interest, but they couldn't get enough evidence. You want to know how they decided to question him?"

"Sure."

"They took his photograph at the fire scene—a fire in 1971 in the Northend, one of the Mercer properties."

"How'd they get a picture of him?"

"That's something a lot of people don't know. Most firebugs come around to watch the fires they've set. That's why it's standard practice for fire department photographers to take pictures of the crowd as well as the fire. Patrick was in the crowd."

"Weird." I was feeling pretty good—knowing now I could go on with my crummy little cab-driving life.

Deirdre was not connected to anything criminal. For the most part she remained out of the newspapers.

She did fire Sheila Woo, ostensibly for releasing the firm's confidential information. Sheila was happy to go to another outfit, one which happens to be close to my place so that I can drive by and visit on my way to work.

I went back to driving cab and had no further contact with lawyers. My yellow pages advertising lapsed.

I saw Chicken Man one more time. I had not been able to convince Garcia to drop the warrant for him, so I was kind of expecting the visit.

It was early in the morning, still dark out, when I got off work at the cab lot and he came to see me. I was standing at the edge of the lighted compound, smoking a cigarette, taking deep breaths to see if I could exorcise my recent depression and guilt. I had been thinking about Walter Egan a lot lately. He had saved my life and he had died in a fire that was set to kill me. I knew it wasn't something I could have controlled, but I still felt guilty. I had been through this kind of guilt before so it was a familiar depression and guilt. By my standards, I could have been considered to be in a pretty good mood.

Out of the corner of my eye I spotted a hulking figure sneaking up behind me. I was pretty sure it was Chicken Man, playing the bully again. When he was about three feet away I spun around, swung my left arm as hard as I could, and brought my fist up into his soft solar plexus. He grunted and sat hard on the ground.

"What the hell did you do that for?" he moaned.

"Why the hell were you sneaking up on me?"

"I just don't like you, man," he said finally. "I was planning on giving you a hug goodbye before I left. Because of you, I gotta leave town."

I helped him to his feet and then to his truck, half a block away. He climbed in on the driver's side and I took a seat on the passenger side. He was returning to his normal self, mean and surly.

"Man, I ought to beat you up," he said. He wasn't much for making pleasant conversation. He was like most bullies, he wanted to beat you up whether he liked you or not. It was his way of relating.

"C'mon, Chicken Man. I've been trying to clear you. That's what you wanted."

"Jesus, I wish I had a joint."

"Feel lucky you're not in the joint."

"Some joke. You got any dope?"

"I have some speed," I told him, getting an idea that fit my mood. For some reason I was remembering the corduroy suit jacket I had at home. The one without front pockets. "It's new. They call it Orange Wind."

"Hey, let's have some."

I pulled the vial from my pocket and gave him six pills from it. They were dark-orange 100-milligram tablets of Thorazine. He took them and swallowed them like candy. It's good he didn't chew on them, because they taste like hell and he'd have spit them out. I wouldn't have misled most people this way, but it just seemed like the right therapy for Chicken Man. In a few minutes he would be safe as a kitten. He would have a drug lobotomy. He would be indifferent to almost everything and his muscles would be like lead. Inside, his mind would be screaming that something was wrong. It would last from eight to twelve hours. If he was lucky, he would sleep part of the time.

Good old Thorazine.

"Is that guy still in a coma?" he asked, looking straight out the window, concentrating on how he was feeling, waiting for the dope to hit.

"Yeah. He weighed 120 pounds at last measurement."

"Veggie time," he said.

"Yeah."

We sat there for quite a while without speaking until I figured he was safely under the weather. When I talked to him, all he could reply was "Huh?"

I started climbing out of the cab of the truck as he struggled with some final statement. I waited for it.

"Man, I feel heavy," he said, after long effort.

"You're overweight. What would you expect?" I said, and slammed the door of the old pickup. That would teach him to ruin my new suit.

My life is much quieter now. I regularly spend time with Allison. I date Sheila. I am considering a more sedate career—perhaps as an accountant. I don't dwell as much on Patrick Wills now—who he is, or what he did. At first, after he was hospitalized, I thought about him a lot—imagined his crimes and his sick relationships, so I could feel more sure of the justice of his present condition. I still wonder if he dreams now, if he has demons, demons of the sort that haunted me. If so, he is truly in hell.

I have also made some peace with my mother and the friend who died in Vietnam. It was a mild insult to their memories to have conjured them up as ghosts, so I visit the place they actually reside now. It happens that both of their graves are located in a small cemetery in the north end of the city, near where we lived when I was a little boy. I go there regularly now and I try to remember them as they were when they were alive—not as my mind had resurrected them.

And though I have recovered, I have been affected in many ways. And so has my daughter, small as she is, far as she was from the center of the storm. When I visited her the other day she was lying very still on the couch with her eyes closed and her arms folded across her chest. It made me uneasy, so I asked her what she was doing.

"Sometimes I like to pretend I'm dead," she said.

"I know what you mean," I told her, lifting her off the couch. "But there will be plenty of time for that. Right now let's see if we can find a swing set."

As her father it's important for me to show her how to get out of these moods.